Valerie

Valerie

Bruce Dulany

gatekeeper press™
Columbus, Ohio

VALERIE

Published by **Gatekeeper Press**

2167 Stringtown Rd, Suite 109

Columbus, OH 43123-2989

www.GatekeeperPress.com

Library of Congress Control Number: 2021953495

ISBN (paperback): 9781662924408

eISBN: 9781662924415

Table of Contents

Part Three

THE INVISIBLE GIRL 119

Part One

THE
BEST DAY
EVER

Be Our Guest

"Hey Mom, I'm bored" stated a confused Valerie. "Why can't I go to school? I miss my friends and teachers at Hallsberry School. I miss singing in music class with Ms. Ariana, I miss playing scatter ball in gym class with Ms. Penelope and I miss playing soccer with Mr. Dulany. I especially miss being with my teacher Mrs. Marino. Did you know she is pregnant? I don't know if her baby is the size of an apple, a cantaloupe, or a watermelon. Maybe she had her baby!"

"Did I do something wrong? Am I being punished? You're not even letting me go outside to play with my friends!" cried a very angry Valerie. "What is going on?" Valerie's Mom just smiled at her and gently gave her a giant hug. As Mom hugged her sweet daughter she whispered in Valerie's ear "I love you sweetheart. But I don't think you are old enough to understand what is going on. It's very scary, even for me and your father. For now, just enjoy this time home with your family."

Valerie's Mom kissed her on the forehead and told Valerie to go to her room and play. Being a well-mannered young lady who respected her mother and father, Valerie did as she was told. Unhappy, and confused, Valerie went to her small bedroom. As she grabbed the bronze handle of the large white wooden door, Valerie stood there and wondered what was really going on in this world.

Mrs. Marino and Mr. Dulany, as well as all the teachers, had always taught and encouraged the students at Hallsberry School to ask questions. No matter how silly, no matter how small the question, no matter how embarrassing, when you had a question, ask. That's how you learn. Taking a deep breath, Valerie turned around and bravely returned to the living room where her Mother was texting on her smartphone.

Seeing her daughter return did not please Valerie's Mom. "I thought I told you to go to your room!" Respectfully, Valerie started to talk. "I am old enough to take care of my sister Vivian, when you go out to the grocery store, I am old enough to take the bus to school, by myself, I am old enough to go to 7-11 to buy milk, by myself. Why am I not old enough to know why I am being quarantined in my own house?"

Realizing her sweet daughter was growing up faster than she ever had imagined. Valerie's Mom hung up her phone. She looked Valerie straight in the eyes and asked her what questions she had. Taking another deep breath, Valerie thought hard. What is a pandemic? What is Covid-19?

With the help of the internet, Valerie's Mom explained to Valerie that a pandemic was a disease that covered a large region of area. Covid-19 was a very serious virus. Some of the symptoms included fever, coughing and shortness of breath. Valerie who was very confused now, told her Mom "Vivian is not sick, Dad is not showing any of these symptoms, you are not sick, and I can honestly say I have never felt better. So, I can go outside? Can I go to school?"

Smiling, her Mother said "It's more complicated than that. Healthy people can carry the disease, show no symptoms but pass it to the more vulnerable. Vulnerable means weaker. Older people, like Grandma and Grandpa, sick people like Mr. Dulany are more easily susceptible to the disease. And like stronger, healthy people who are more likely to fight off the disease, their immune systems can't fight it as well.

Is that why Grandma and Grandpa are staying inside too? Is that we you dropped groceries on their front porch last Saturday? Do you think Mr. Dulany is staying protected inside his house? Asked a very concerned Valerie. Overwhelmed with questions Valerie's Mom answered a very solemn Yes! Yes! And yes! Everybody needs to stay home so the disease does not continue to spread.

Valerie heard her Mom say something about social distancing. Mystified, Valerie asked "What is social distancing?" Social distancing is where people always stay six feet apart. No hugging, no high fives, no fist pumping. No contact. Please honey, you and your sister must remember to wash your hands for at least 20 seconds, with warm water and soap, every few hours. "One of friends at school told me if I just use hand sanitizer I will be fine," proudly stated Valerie.

"It's important we follow the facts, not the rumors." Suggested her worried Mom. "Warm water with soap for twenty seconds or more is the best, followed by a squirt of hand sanitizer is the best solution. Try and keep your hands away from your face, mouth and eyes."

Rumors, Valerie had been hearing a lot of these lately. The news stations, the internet, her friends on Facebook all had something bad to say about the Covid-19 virus. Starvation, the end of the world, chaos in the streets, never going back to school, these were just a few things she heard. What was true? What was a rumor? What was fact? What was fiction? Confused and bewildered, Valerie looked at her Mom for answers.

Saddened by Valerie's anxiety, her Mom told her the whole family would stay off the internet, Facebook and stop watching the news for a while. All they were doing were causing anxiety and stress in her precious family. Not wanting to lie to her daughter, she did tell Valerie she would keep checking these places every morning on updates on the situation. However, Valerie and her sister Vivian were not to go on the internet or on any social media pages until further notice.

PART ONE

Starting to understand the seriousness of the situation, Valerie smiled and asked when it will all be over. Her mother grinned and told her precious daughter that the quarantine or stay at home order would not be lifted for at least another month. Valerie's smiled turned into a frown. Disappointed, Valerie asked "Another month in lock down?" Then Valerie ran to her room, slammed the door, hid underneath her blankets and started to cry.

Her younger sister Vivian, who was reading Valerie's favorite book *"The Mountain meets the Moon"*, stopped and was intrigued by her sister hiding. Although two years apart in age, they were almost like twins. They both had the same hairstyles they were both straight A students and they both had the most beautiful smiles. Valerie and Vivian loved spending time together and they both loved sharing a room together. The two were often thought of like Lilo and Stitch, Liv and Maddie or Anna and Elsa, two peas in a pod.

Trying to be considerate, but also trying to be compassionate, Vivian slowly approached her crying sister. "Do you want to talk about it?" she sweetly whispered. Valerie did not respond but Vivian knew something was wrong. Although Vivian was quiet away from home, she loved to talk at home, and she knew how to make her sister laugh.

Stealing a scene from one of their favorite Disney movies, "Beauty and the Beast", Vivian started with a simple but highly effective comment "Young lady. It is with high honor and greatest pleasure that we welcome you this morning". Valerie stuck her head out of the pile of blankets, with a colossal smile she said "Really?" Their Mother announced breakfast will be ready in five minutes.

Continuing trying to uplift her sister's spirits Vivian restarted her presentation, "Young lady. It is with deepest pride and greatest pleasure that we welcome you this morning. Let us pull up a chair as our bedroom proudly presents your newest adventures during this temporary crisis. Be my sister, be my sister. Put our friendship to the test!" Valerie came out of her cocoon and gave Vivian the biggest hug ever. Valerie wiped her tear-soaked face and responded, "I don't care what I say about you, you are the best sister I have!"

Breakfast
of Champions

Then from the small kitchen their Mom announced "breakfast is ready! Girls, wash your hands and come down for breakfast." Smelling the wonderful scent in the air, the girls still in their princess pajamas stampeded down the carpeted stairs, washed, for 20 seconds, and sanitized their hands and quietly sat down at the large wooden table, awaiting their breakfast.

It didn't take long before their mother came to the table carrying a huge pile of Eggo Waffles, freshly toasted. Extremely excited, Vivian exclaimed "Mom you haven't made these in ages!" Swiftly Vivian grabbed three of the waffles off the stack, buttered the beauties, then grabbed the bottle of pure Vermont maple syrup and generously poured the liquid gold on top of Mt. St. Delicious. Without an ounce of hesitation, she attacked the pile of waffles. "You look like a hungry crocodile when the gazelles try and cross the river." Laughed Valerie.

Overhearing their conversation, their Mom told them she was going to be home with them until this situation was over. "Does that mean you are going to start cooking again?" eagerly asked Valerie. "Mom, does that mean you are going to start making your homemade enchiladas? Your homemade lasagna? Your delicious nachos piled high with cheddar cheese, sour cream and your freshly made guacamole topped with thinly sliced jalapeno peppers? Curiously asked the younger Vivian.

Drooling with anticipation of Mom cooking again, Valerie silently wondered if she would cook her favorite dish soon. Overcome with temptation, Valerie suddenly blurted out "I love your chicken alfredo! I could eat it every night!" Pausing for a minute Valerie prolonged her comments. "Love your cooking, really do, but I hope we can still visit Panda Express once in a while!"

Mom just smiled at her sweet girls. "Since I will be home with you girls too, I will plan on keeping busy also. I will catch up on all the cleaning, maybe you girls could help me?" The girls pretended they didn't hear their mother and continued to scarf down the delicious Eggo waffles, doused with the golden syrup from the northeast. "Selective hearing?" the Mom quietly asked. "And yes, I will bring out my pots and pans, I will bring out my oven mitts and will turn on the oven for something besides pizza." Proudly announced Mom. The girls tried to remain quiet, but the urge was too much to handle. Simultaneously, Vivian and Valerie screamed "Yeah!!" And ran up and hugged their mother.

Still holding her precious daughters tightly, Mom took a moment and reminded the girls that this time at home was not going to be spent watching television, however watching a National Geographic episode once a day would be allowed. "I love those shows!" Exclaimed Vivian. "Especially the ones about the migrating elephants in Africa." Valerie chimed in touting she preferred watching Animal Planet, specifically the shows about helping lost, abused dogs.

Today, the mom politely requested, "I would like you to first do the homework that you teachers told you to do on the laptops that Hallsberry School gave you. Valerie make sure you are helping your sister you know she has such a hard time with math." "Since when?" replied Valerie. Her sweet daughters started to bolt out of the room, "Hold on young ladies!" the Mom announced. The girls stopped dead in their tracks. "When you are done with your homework, I want you to clean your room"

"But Mom?" whined the younger sister Vivian. "I know where everything is!" Not accepting the answer, the Mom quickly responded "Empty water bottles on the floor? Dresses on the floor? Used bath towels all over the room?" "We have all been busy, this down time will be a great time to catch up on cleaning, a little at a time. However," the girls sighed, they never liked when Mom said that bad, bad word, however. "However, as you clean, make a list of everything you could possibly do inside our home. Be realistic, Vivian please do not put down swimming with the dolphins and Valerie please don't put on your list driving lessons in a Pink Porsche! Save that one for the boys!"

Disgusted, both the girls answered her with a big "YUK! Boys have cooties! Despondent, the girls went to their room and immediately grabbed their laptops and started on their homework. After a few minutes Vivian looked at Valerie and exclaimed "We are going to die!" dramatically she continued "We are going to die a slow painful death." Coughing and holding her throat, she plunged to her bed. What could possibly be her last words, she uttered out "OF BOREDOM!"

Hearing the giant thud, their Mom called up "Is everything okay girls?" Valerie responded, "Vivian is being dramatic again." Mom responded "Vivian, maybe you should give up the violin and get into theater. After a few hours, the girls were almost done with their homework. The girls decided to start by cleaning their closet. The closet of doom. Why? asked a very lazy Vivian. "Why don't we watch tv all day? Why don't we take naps?" Vivian calmly asked.

"Considering you are so smart you really don't act like it." Valerie said. "Why, did I have to be the first born? All the responsibility, all the brains, all the good looks! It's just not fair!" Vivian got angry, "Take that back! Or

I'm telling Mom! You called me stupid and ugly!" Vivian started to call for Mom when Valerie jumped across the bed and covered her mouth. As they struggled they both fell off the bed and created another even larger thud.

"What's going on now?" called a very concerned Mom. Both the girls looked at each other and started to laugh. Vivian now laughing quickly answered "I am just being dramatic again." On the floor Valerie noticed the many empty water bottles. "Doesn't Mr. Dulany collect plastic lids for the cancer society? And he uses the bottom of the bottle to start seedlings inside his basement. Picking up an old soda can Vivian reminded Valerie that Ms. Samantha saves the tabs for cancer research. "And" Valerie continued "we can save the paper tubes from toilet paper and paper towels for Ms. Bhavya." Vivian smiled as they collected the wanted items.

Not wanting to be outdone by her older sister Valerie, Vivian reminded her sweet sister about box tops and Campbell soup labels. Valerie was impressed with her younger sister. "It's kind of cool, without doing much we are really helping out many people. A little kindness goes a long way!" Valerie proclaimed.

As Vivian collected the empty water bottles and lids, the paper tubes from the bathroom and the tabs from soda cans she asked Valerie "What are we going to do with this stuff?" Valerie thought for a moment, "Open the closet, there should be an old shoe box in there we could use." Vivian was mystified, "The closet?" she asked very dramatically." We haven't opened the closet in years!"

Valerie knew Vivian was right, they hadn't open it for a while. Valerie's imagination began to run wild, but then she thought to herself "How bad can it be? Blood sucking bats? Man eating zombies? Hideous clowns?" Trying to hide the fear in her face, Valerie told Vivian "Go ahead, don't be afraid, it will be okay. Trying to be the brave little sister, Vivian grabbed the round brass handle.

3

Lunch in Yellowstone Park

Suddenly, the voice of heaven called "Lunch! Lunch is ready!" Like hungry wolves chasing their prey, Vivian and Valerie bolted down the long staircase into the dining room. Proudly the younger athletic Vivian bragged she had won the race. Stopping cold in their tracks, there was no lunch, no dishes on the table and no Mom. They stood there frozen, not knowing what to do. "Girls, where are you? Your lunch is getting cold!" asked their Mom. Continuing one room over was the living room where their sweet mother set up lunch on the coffee table, which was in front of the 55" 4k ultra tv.

"All right!" exclaimed Valerie. "We can watch all three Descendants movies!" Vivian knew better. "I have picked out a National Geographic special called Wild Yellowstone. Learn while you eat," said Mom. The girls looked at their lunch, apple juice, carrots with ranch dressing, a small bag of Takis, a small cheeseburger and for dessert, one snack size bag of Oreos.

Hesitantly, their Mom paused for a moment. "Remember girls, many families are having a hard time putting food on the table, please be thankful that we can still do that as a family. Let's make sure we are not wasting any food."

"We need some groceries from Jewel" bashfully announced their Mom. "Valerie you are naturally in charge, eat lunch, watch the show, finish your homework for the day and start cleaning your room, including that closet. I will back in an hour said their Mom. "Can you get some rocky road ice cream?" screamed Vivian. Valerie knew better, politely she calmly asked, "please mom could you please get some more Takis?"

Thinking about the families who could not afford groceries, Valerie ran to her coin jar on top of her dresser. With her small hands she scooped up a handful of coins and gave them to her mom. "Buy some food for the food bank!" Vivian declared. Mom smiled. Not to be outdone, Vivian did the same.

"Girls, I will do my best." Her mother said quietly. "I need to stock up on the essentials". Confused, Vivian asked "what's an essential?" Trying to show how smart she was Valerie quickly raised her hand screaming "I know! I know" without waiting for the approval to go on, Valerie kept talking "it's the important things you can't live without like toilet paper, milk, eggs, bread and meat."

"That's correct!" proudly replied Mom. "Vivian can you think of any essentials?" Vivian thought hard for a second, smiled at her Mom and gracefully said "Yes I can...... Takis and Rocky Road ice cream!" Trying to contain her laughter Mom nonchalantly turned her back. "I have to go, be back in an hour. Remember when you get done eating your lunch, cleanup and start cleaning your room." Starting to chuckle Mom swiftly turned her back and said, "Call me if there is a problem" she rapidly opened the large brown front door and exited saying those magic words "Love You!"

Quickly, Valerie took charge. She demanded Vivian give her the bag of Oreo's. Vivian was oblivious. Vivian was hypnotized about the wolves at Yellowstone. As Vivian dipped her crisp carrot sticks into the creamy ranch dressing she totally ignored Valerie's outburst of trying to be mean to her sweet little sister. Sensing her imminent defeat of trying to be a bully, Valerie sat down and finished her cheeseburger, but wondered how bullies stay mean for so long, it was exhausting. It was much easier to be nice.

Sitting down, Valerie decided she would watch the special on the wolves with her sister. Vivian was amazed how the wolves acted in the Yellowstone Park. They lived together. They protected each other. They hunted together. They ate together. No matter what happened, no matter the extreme cold of the harsh winters or the intense heat in the summer from the blazing sun in Yellowstone Park, the wolves stuck together. They were all in this together. Vivian was moved by the sentiment and bashfully asked her sister if their family was all in this together.

Valerie didn't hesitate to answer, "Remember in Lilo and Stitch? They use the word Ohana. Remember what Ohana means?" Thinking for a moment Valerie hesitantly answered "Family, Ohana means family. Family means nobody is left behind or forgotten."

"Excellent answer!" Valerie replied "Of course, our family is in this together." Trying not to show her fear, Vivian hugged her older sister for comfort. It was a long hug, but Valerie knew she needed Vivian as much as Vivian needed her. The credits for the Yellow Stone special soon started to appear, signaling an unannounced end to their special moment.

Looking at each other they started to laugh, seeing a tear in her sweet sister's eye, she lovingly wiped the tear from her cheek. Not saying a word, they turned off the television, and cleaned up their dishes and cups from the delicious lunch that their sweet Mom had made for them. Lighting the mood, Valerie called "Last one up to our room, is a rotten egg!". With a sudden bolt of athleticism, Vivian darted past Valerie screaming "wouldn't want to be you!"

Together they both reached the small bedroom together. As they pushed the door open, they were appalled, appalled at the mess. For some reason they never saw it before, clothes on the floor, old homework crumbled and scattered throughout the room, the small princess trash can was still overflowing with empty water bottles and half-drunk sparkling water cans. Valerie thought to herself, "maybe this situation is making us grow up a little faster."

Vivian reluctantly volunteered to sprint back downstairs and get a garbage bag, or two. As Vivian bent down in the cabinet drawer, she heard something repeatedly bang and bump their back door. Terrified, Vivian tried to call Valerie, but nothing came out of her mouth. The monster grunted and groaned banging against the door. Finally, Valerie came marching down the stairs, asking her fearful sister "Why didn't you open the door for Mom, her arms are filled with groceries, didn't you see the text message from Mom?"

Ashamed, Vivian quickly opened the door and grabbed two large shopping bags from her mother's overstuffed hands. Remorseful, Vivian put down the black garbage bags on the kitchen counter and said, "I'm sorry Mom" and grabbed two more bags from her mother's small hands. Trying to understand everything her young daughter was going through, their mom just smiled.

Valerie noticed how embarrassed Vivian was, she needed to escape. Thinking quick, Valerie asked her Mom if they could take Kiara for a walk. "He hasn't been out since this morning" Valerie blurted out. "Excuse me, young lady," her Mom quickly responded. "Sorry Mom," Valerie said in a milder tone. "Can Vivian and I please take Kiara for a walk to the park? I think we all need some fresh air."

Realizing the gravity of the situation, Vivian's embarrassment, their Mom paused for a moment, "That's fine, finish putting away the groceries when you come back. Did you ever finish your room?" Their sweet Mom continued, "please change out of your Princess pajamas, what will our neighbors think?" Please, please remember our discussion on social distancing!"

Unsure of what her mother meant Vivian bashfully asked, "social distancing?" Valerie quickly replied "Social distancing is where you keep at least six feet apart, no handshakes, no high fives, no fist pumps and no hugs with other people. You can say hi, but that's all." They quickly changed, put Kiara on a leash and flew out the back door.

Vivian was very quiet as usual, but when she got to the park she couldn't stop talking. "Thank you, Valerie, for saving me, to be perfectly honest, I was so scared when I heard noises at the door." Repeating herself she continued bravely, "I was scared at the door, and I am............ scared about this whole Covid-19 situation!"

Valerie hesitated for a moment, thinking of the right thing to say. Comforting her sister, she lovingly replied "WE are all scared, WE are all worried, but WE are all in this together, WE have your back! I promise." Vivian smiled and replied, "Ohana!" Suddenly they heard lightning.

"Come on Kiara, come on Vivian, we must get home before.... "Then without warning the storm clouds let loose and dumped a torrential rainstorm on the young dog walkers, soaking them to the bone. Grabbing Vivian's hand and grabbing the cold wet leash, Valerie quickly raced the short distance to their home, fighting the cold blinding rain and trying to avoid the many over-flowing puddles.

Finally reaching home, the rain-soaked trio were warmly welcomed by their concerned Mom who was holding several fresh from the dryer warm bath towels. "Go upstairs and get out of these wet clothes" ordered their Mom. "I was impatient, so I put away the rest of the groceries from Jewel. Then I went upstairs to help you with your room, but I say this lovingly, but it was atrocious, disgusting, hideous..." Vivian cut in "Okay, Mom we get it! It's messy!"

Seeing her older sister Valerie shivering, Vivian stepped up and grabbed the big black garbage bags she originally took out before her Mom came home from grocery shopping, then she grabbed Valerie's cold hand. "Don't worry sis, this time I got you!" Encouraged the two began their journey upstairs.

"As long as you are going upstairs, can you bring the Colgate toothpaste and shampoo to the upstairs bathroom?" asked Mom. Slightly confused, and still shivering, Valerie challenged her mother "Weren't you going to get Charmin toilet paper and lavender hand sanitizer for the upstairs bathroom?"

Impressed with her daughter's memory Mom respectfully replied, "If only you would remember dates for your history tests. But yes, I was going to get Charmin bath tissue, napkins, hand sanitizer, bottled water, and bleach, but people were going crazy. The shelves were empty. I looked and we should have enough for a couple days, nothing to worry about."

The girls took the Colgate toothpaste and the TRESemme' thick and creamy salon shampoo upstairs and quickly dried off and changed into some fresh pajamas. Valerie picked out her grey Koala bear hooded pajama outfit with footsies and Vivian proudly pulled out her Unicorn onesie with the ever so unique rainbow horn.

Vivian explained to Valerie that the rainbow horn was magical. Pacifying her younger sister, Valerie exclaimed "That is so awesome! How does it work?" Sharing her vast knowledge of unicorns Vivian unleashed an avalanche of facts and interesting things about unicorns. Taking a deep breath, Vivian started "Did you know that unicorns can only be seen by believers? Did you know that each unicorn eats only a certain type of candy? Did you know that unicorns sleep on clouds made of cotton candy? Did you know unicorns poop rainbow sprinkles?"

Valerie quickly stopped her sister, "EEWWW! TMI! too much information!" Vivian continued, "But the rainbow horn represents protection, not only for me, but for my whole family, You, me, Mom and Dad. Protection from evil, from sickness, from bullies, from all that is bad in this world!" Valerie smiled at her sweet sister, then replied "Even when Dad tries and makes us breakfast on Saturday Mornings?"

Vivian laughed uncontrollably. "Hey, I heard that!" said a deep voice before tapping on their door. "Dads Home!" exclaimed the girls simultaneously as they both rushed the door to give their Dad a huge hug. Juggling a platter of breaded chicken tenders with ranch dressing and celery sticks their Dad expertly balanced the afternoon snack for his sweet daughters while he hugged them right back.

Snack Time

Confused, but being brave, Vivian politely asked their Dad why he was home so early. He usually came home just before dinner time. Not knowing their previous conversation with Mom, Dad inadvertently told them they were too young to understand. Vivian proudly proclaimed, "Mom said we were old enough to understand and Mom promised to tell us everything!"

Baffled, Dad looked down the staircase at Mom for clarification. All Mom did was nod her head, agreeing with what his precious little girls had said. "Please let me put these down! Mom gave them to me to bring them up for you for an afternoon snack. She said you were busy "cleaning" your room." Looking around at the mess, he politely said "I don't see the "cleaning".

Hungry, Vivian grabbed the plate from her Dad and like the hungry lion catching its unsuspecting prey, Vivian started to devour the delectable chicken tenders. Trying to avoid an uncomfortable situation Dad started to leave. With a mouth full of chicken tenders, Vivian mumbled something. All Dad could say was "What?" Valerie quickly interpreted, "that's Vivian for why are you home early?"

Dad was caught, his sweet daughters were growing up. He told them that the governor asked businesses to have workers work from home if possible. Their Dad continued saying his boss gave him permission to work from home as long as he did the work. Vivian interrupted their Dad and said "It's like us working from home with our computers from the school. Maybe, tomorrow we all can sit downstairs in the office and work together?"

Impressed beyond imagination, Dad developed a tear in his eye. "That would be awesome!" exclaimed Dad. Seeing the tear in Dad's eye, Valerie leaned over and gave Dad an enormous hug, followed by Vivian. Coming from the hallway and seeing everything, Mom came in crying and announcing, "Group Hug!" Taking control of the situation little Vivian smiled and retorted "WE ARE all in this together!"

Extremely proud of their daughters Dad agreed. But with a sense of humor, Mom debated being all in this together regarding cleaning the girl's room. Mom abruptly said, "You made the mess, you clean the mess." Not saying another word both the Mom and Dad left the room, grabbing the empty dinner plate that once was covered with chicken tenders.

Taking their Mom very seriously, Valerie reminded Vivian they needed to clean their room, starting with their closet. Sarcastically, Valerie asked her tiny sister "Are you hungry? I'm famished!" the completely naïve Vivian reminded Valerie dinner would be ready in three hours.

Collecting every ounce of courage in her tiny body, Vivian went to the small closet and grabbed the brass doorknob handle. "Here goes nothing!" she timidly said to herself. Then she heard two knocks on a door. Completely frightened, she asked Valerie "Did you hear that?"

The brave sister stepped forward and proudly proclaimed "Let me get the door!" With a smile on her face Valerie went to the bedroom door and deliberately opened it very slowly. Shivering with fear, Vivian hid behind her bed watching her brave sister. Suddenly, being humorous and a tiny bit mean Valerie quickly opened-up the bedroom door. Screaming "It's Dad!"

Vivian quickly scooted under the bed. Then she smelled it, more chicken tenders, fresh hot juicy breaded chicken tenders. Vivian was transfixed, the smell was tantalizing. Forgetting her fear, she slowly got herself from under the bed and approached the new plate of chicken. "Is everything okay girls? Dad asked. The girls shook their heads yes. "Valerie, these are for you. Mom has got your back; she knows Vivian ate the whole first plate." Dad handed Valerie the plate, with two bottles of apple juice and went back downstairs. Vivian hung her head, saddened by the whole situation.

Vivian went back to the closet door, trying to forget about the warm juicy chicken tenders that her sister was now enjoying. "Oh, get over here!" Valerie told her sister. Vivian grabbed three tenders and a bottle of apple juice to wash it all down. "You are the best sister ever!" Vivian smiled and returned the compliment, "Right back at you!"

Finally, relaxed, Vivian slowly turned the door handle and opened it slightly, nothing. No bats no birds, no spiders, no lions, and no zombies. Full of confidence, she skooched the closet door open a few more inches but nothing, no scary teachers, no mean recess supervisors, and no strict principal. Feeling totally invincible Vivian swung the door wide open, but nothing, no dodgeballs, no extra homework, and no obnoxious boys.

Claiming victory, the unicorn clad young lady turned around and raised her raised her hooves as a premature gesture of a victorious celebration. Knowing their Dad was now working from home, Vivian started singing "We are the greatest, we are the greatest of the world." In celebration of overcoming her sister overcoming her fear, Valerie started a slow clap. That's when it happened, the humongous stack of unwanted toys, books and assorted items leaned to the front, leaned to the back and lean forward one last time.

Valerie foresaw the future. Speechless, from fear, Valerie tried to save her sister yet again. However, Valerie's legs did not move, they were frozen in time. Immobilized, all she could do was watch in horror as the huge pile fell, toppled off the unicorn's horn and scattered randomly in front of

Vivian. After what seemed hours but was really a few seconds Valerie was finally able to move, Valerie rushed to the aid of her sister. "Are you okay?" Then from downstairs Mom yelled "Is everything okay?"

Pausing for a moment, the sisters looked at each other and abruptly yelled "Everything is okay, Mom." Then there was complete silence. Whispering quietly, Valerie asked her sister, "Seriously, are you okay?" Vivian stood there smiling from ear to ear. "I'm wearing the rainbow unicorn horn, nothing can hurt me now, Nothing!

Perplexed, astonished and totally awakened with the realization of the power of the horn, Valerie realized that the Unicorn horn worked and promised herself that when it was time to get new pajamas, she would pick unicorn pajamas with a hoodie that had a rainbow horn. They would be on top of her Christmas list, top of her birthday wish-list and top of her Flag Day list. If possible, she would clean out the garage for extra money, or if she were desperate enough she would clean the bathrooms, anything to get a pair of the unicorn pajamas with the magical rainbow horn.

Daydreaming, Valerie thought about wearing the powerful pajamas and the possibilities for fame and fortune. Stopping bullies from teasing her good friend Evelyn, stopping the boys from excluding her and other girls from soccer, stopping other students from making fun and her and her friend Trudy from being smart and trying to learn at Hallsberry School. She would be known as Unicorn Girl.

Continuing to dream, Valerie thought about the movies and graphic novels they would make about her adventures. Lilo and Valerie, Finding Valerie, Valerie and the Beast, the possibilities would be endless. She continued to dream about the books her favorite author Mr. Dulany would write about her, The Unicorn who Saved Christmas, Unicorn Wars; Valerie saves the Universe and possibly the best story that ever could be written, The Autobiography of Valerie, the Greatest Unicorn to have ever galloped on the planet Earth. Money would be endless, fame would be limitless, and life would be grand. Valerie just sat there and smiled.

Suddenly, she heard Vivian yelling at her. "Aren't you going to help? Are you daydreaming again? Grossed out at the possibility Valerie liking a boy, Valerie accusatorily asked her sister "You're not thinking about that boy in your class again, what's his name Joey?"

Ignoring her immature sister, Valerie quickly apologized and started to help clean-up the mess. "It looks like Mt. Saint Unwanted Stuff threw up!" complained Vivian. "We should have a garage sale!" replied Valerie. "No!" sarcastically answered Vivian "We need some garbage bags!"

As they succumbed to their Mom's wishes of cleaning their room, the two sisters quietly organized the barf from Mt Saint Unwanted Stuff. One pile was Valerie's pile for a summer garage sale and the other pile was for Vivian's Friday garbage pickup. Picking up an old notebook from Ms. Crystal's advanced math class, Vivian asked "Keep it? Or Garbage?" Obviously keep it! Declared Valerie.

The afternoon hours flew by with the girls, the barf from Mt Saint Unwanted Stuff was diminishing. The girl's childhood memories were being categorized, keep or throw way. Vivian wondered "Is this what life boils down to?" Valerie suddenly burst out "Look this is a picture you drew in first grade in Ms. Mia's art class." Valerie continued to stare at it "Girl, you got talent! Vivian, think about a career in art."

"Oh, no!" exclaimed Vivian. "Look at the garbage pile!" Thinking the worst, Valerie turned herself around "Where is it?" Vivian quickly said, "It's the stack with the old chewing gum stuck to your C-math quiz, some old school weekly reminders from Ms. Frida's first grade class and your diary from a few years ago."

The Diary

Appalled, Valerie asked Vivian. "Why are we throwing it away?" The comedic Vivian intentionally sidelined the obvious concern. "The C-math quiz, or is the weekly reminders?" "You are such a little brat!" hysterically answered Valerie. "Give me my diary!" she demanded.

Vivian rudely opened the private life of Valerie. Curious about the secrets that her sister held, Vivian bravely opened the diary. Valerie was fuming, "Don't you dare!" she sternly warned. Taunting her older sister, Vivian stood as she would be doing a presentation in Ms. Brianna's class. Clearing her throat and looking at her target audience, Valerie, Vivian started "March 1, today." Angrily, Valerie warned her sister again.

Vivian cleared her throat and started her presentation again. "I'm warning you!" Valerie threatened. Vivian ignored her red-faced sister, "March 1", she repeated. "Today we had" "Enough!" demanded Valerie, then without hesitation she charged. Raving mad, she went straight at Vivian determined to stop her evil sister from reading anymore of her private diary.

Valerie liked writing her in diary. At the end of every day, she would write about the day. Valerie started doing this when she was in Ms. Kadence's second grade class. Ms. Kadence would give her extra paw prints for writing. The tradition continued in Ms. Samantha's third grade class and Mrs. Maria's fourth grade class. Although she was in Mrs. Marino class, Valerie had Mr. Syed for creative writing and like all the teachers at Hallsberry School she encouraged Valerie to continue writing in her diary.

But the diary included all her private thoughts and private feelings. Private was the key word. As she rushed her little sister, Valerie gained speed. However, the little Vivian was very athletic, she darted to the left, she darted to the right thwarting her sister's awkward anger. "Come on old lady!" Vivian jested. Getting angrier by the second, Valerie took a deep breath and jumped at Vivian. Vivian was quick, quick enough to avoid the attempted pounce.

Valerie landed on her bed, missing Vivian by a mile. Discouraged, defeated and completely out of breath, Valerie put up the proverbial white flag, she gave up. Preparing to be humiliated, Valerie dramatically announced "I believe we have relatives in Alaska, send my mail there."

With an evil victorious grin, Vivian restarted her presentation. "In case you forgot, Mr. Ethan always said I was reading two grades higher, so your fancy big words are not going to phase me one bit!" Completely exhausted, Valerie pleaded with Vivian to quit torturing her, "Just read it!" begging "Please, just read it!"

Vivian was smiling, the rainbow unicorn horn worked again. Daydreaming, Vivian thought about the power of the horn. "No more recess outside on cold days, no more of those nasty French toast sticks for lunch, I will be Mr. D's helper every day, and there is nothing anybody can do about! Nothing!" she diabolically thought.

Tired of being tortured, Valerie grabbed last year's diary from her vicious sister's cold hands. Frustrated, Valerie started to read the story out loud, "March 1. Today was a school snow day. Mom took my sister and I to the hill at Camera Park. It was too cold for Mom, she stayed in the car the whole time, listening to Mexican music on the radio while watching us from the window. With eight inches of fresh snow on the ground, Vivian and I went down the hill on our rickety wooden sleigh at least 1000 times. IT WAS THE BEST DAY EVER!"

Continuing Valerie wiped a tear from her eye, "We were cold and wet, so after sledding, our sweet Mom took us to McDonald's for some of their rich creamy hot chocolate. Vivian and I both got mini-marshmallows, Mom got something called a Frappuccino, IT WAS AWESOME! When we finally got home, Dad helped us take our mattresses off the bed and he made us a castle with bed sheets and blankets. We played games all night long, talked and watched one off our favorite movies, "Beauty and the Beast" at least twice, and our other favorite movie "Lilo and Stitch "twice. IT WAS THE BEST DAY EVER! It only ended because Mom told us to be quiet because we were having so much fun!"

Vivian was mortified. "That's all it says?" she whined. "I was hoping for some juicy tidbits of boyfriends, crushes and fairy dust!". Then like a caterpillar coming out of her cocoon, the exhausted Valerie burst into a beautiful Monarch butterfly, fresh with life and energy.

The Butterfly
Tries to Fly

Valerie grabbed the mattress off her bed and dragged it to the center of the room. "What are you doing? "questioned Vivian. Without hesitation, Valerie dumped all of Vivian's stuffed animals of the bed and grabbed Vivian's mattress and haphazardly placed it next to her mattress on the floor. "Don't be so mean, you bruised Mr. Froggy, I think you broke Booboo the Bear's arm, and you threw Willie the Whale out of his aquarium!" complained Vivian.

"Can you please find some tape?" intensely requested Valerie. Remembering how Dad had temporarily fixed the chair leg from her desk last Saturday, Vivian recalled how Mom needed Dad to lift Kiaras fifty-pound bag of Purina puppy chow. Everybody knew you did not leave Mom waiting. Dad left immediately, asking his sweet responsible daughter to put the supplies back in the garage.

The usually responsible Vivian was tired. On that chilly morning Vivian did her usual chores. Taking out the recyclables, emptying out the dishwasher and vacuuming the living room were on top of her "chore" list. Adding another "chore" to her list was unacceptable. Vivian had a playdate, rather a party with Ariel, Belle, Rapunzel, and Cinderella every Saturday afternoon.

PART ONE

This week was no exception, Ariel was going to spill the beans about her relationship with Prince Eric, Rapunzel was coming with a new hairstyle, rumor had it, Cinderella was going to announce a television deal with HGTV about redecorating her castle and Belle was going to keep her informed about the Beast's anger management class. Vivian's party was going to start soon, she still had to get snacks for the party, no time for visiting the garage. Vivian conveniently opened-up the bottom drawer of her antique desk and dumped the hammer, screwdriver, wood glue and grey duct tape into it.

Restless with curiosity, Vivian retrieved the duct tape and asked Valerie, "Why do you need tape?" Showcasing her beautiful smile Valerie proudly declared "for the best day ever". Valerie grabbed a bed sheet and with the help of the fixed desk chair, taped the side of the bedsheet to two of the fan blades from the ceiling fan.

Thinking the worse, Vivian started to cry. "I was only having fun with you; you don't have to split the room in half!" Laughing hysterically, Valerie grabbed Vivian and explained to her she was building a princess castle, just like they used to. Vivian couldn't stop smiling. "We haven't done that in ages!" exclaimed Vivian. Vivian immediately ran over and started to collect things for the princess castle.

"Hold on Princess Vivian!" Valerie declared. "We still need to finish building the castle walls. Picking up the desk chair, Valerie asked Vivian for another bed sheet and two more pieces of the duct tape. "Success!" cried Valerie. Then a piece of the duct tape slipped off the ceiling fan. Staying positive Vivian handed Valerie two more pieces of tape. There was a noise, something happened, something creaked, something snapped, but what? The two continued reinforcing the walls ignoring the creaking and the snapping.

Then the unthinkable happened, the wooden desk chair broke hurling Valerie to the mattresses below. Hearing the loud thud of a body hitting the ground, Mom called up "It sounds like an elephant stampede, is everyone okay?" Laughing quietly at their stupidity, Vivian still wearing her unicorn pajamas found the courage and yelled "Sure Mom, this time it's Valerie being dramatic."

Their Mom didn't believe a word her daughters were saying. Deviously, before going upstairs to spy on the girls, Mom yelled up "Dinner will be ready soon, please be ready." With neither one being hurt with the collapse of the chair the two princesses started filling their castle unaware who was spying on them through the small crack in the door opening.

As their concerned Mom started to peer through the tiny crack in the door, she wondered if she was doing the right thing. She completely trusted her daughters, she trusted them when they cooked her eggs for breakfast, but there was fire. She trusted her girls when they went to the village pool, but there was water. Being a good mother, she let them play soccer at Hallsberry School during recess with Mr. Dulany, but there was the earth. Just two days ago she watched as Vivian and Valerie flew a huge princess kite at Camera park, but there was the air. Over the cold winter they went ice skating and there was ice.

Thinking to herself she asked herself "What kind of terrible mom am I? I have exposed them to the five elements on this hazardous planet, fire, water, earth, air, and ice. I have managed to display my sweet daughters to the perils of this cold earth with no regard for their safety." Worried about her failure as a mother, she knew she had to keep her daughters from the five elements. Stealing a breath of fresh air, she looked through the minute crack.

Peeping through the crack, Mom saw the girls filling their Princess castle. Suddenly, Dad came storming through the small hallway. In passing and carrying a large stack of important papers, their Dad asked their Mom, "Are you spying on the girls again? We have raised them right, please give them their privacy. They know right from wrong! You can trust them!" Dad continued his journey to his home office.

Smiling, Vivian and Valerie's Mom realized the Dad was right. They were good parents they did raise good girls and they knew right from wrong. Taking a small peek, Mom saw the girls struggling to keep the walls up on their make-shift castle. Proud of her young daughters, Mom backed away and worked her way quietly down the stairs to talk with Dad.

Continuing their quest for the best day ever, the girls struggled with the castle walls. As the right side was put up the left side fell. As Valerie fixed the left side, the right side fell. Out of nowhere Mom called "Dinner will be here; I mean dinner will be ready in 30 minutes!". Looking at the small wooden clock on the wall, the girls were determined to have the walls up and the castle decorated within the thirty minutes.

As much as Vivian encouraged her older sister, Valerie, the bedsheets would not stay up. Vivian continued saying "I think you can, I think you can!". Caught in a circle of dismal failure, Valerie sighed and rubbed her red eyes, thinking she was disappointing her sister. The doorbell rang. Immediately, Vivian told Valerie "No matter what, I will always be there for you!"

Dinner Is Served

In the middle of the moment, Mom called "Dinner is ready, wash your hands for twenty seconds and come on down." Like the clock ticking at recess, Vivian went quickly down to the kitchen, leaving only a cloud of smoke. Valerie laughed "Always?" and followed her hungry sister.

As the girls stood in the dining room, they wondered where dinner was, they wondered where Dad was. Suddenly, from the kitchen came Mom carrying two boxes from Mod Pizza. Ecstatic and hungry the lionesses were ready to attack the small herd of gazelles. Purposely stalling, Mom told them to get their laptops, which Mom had conveniently relocated to the living room and show them they did today's homework, before getting the delicious pizza.

The girls were excellent students. Although they were both smart, good grades didn't come easy. Vivian had to practice her math equations daily, addition, subtraction, multiplication and dare I say division. Valerie loved reading, but she struggled with words like justification, vindication, and navigation. Vivian always knew the earth was big and full of different countries but where was Fiji, where was Luxemburg and whoever heard of New Zealand? By the way, where was the old Zealand? Valerie knew about communities but was confused, what is the difference between a road, street, and boulevard?

Whining together, "Mom, the pizza is getting cold, you know we did our homework", the girls looked sympathetically at their Mom. Suddenly, Dad came rumbling down the stairs, "Did you tell the girls the news?" Expecting the worst, Vivian quietly mumbled to Valerie. "Oh No, here it comes!" Valerie quickly looked at Vivian, who was still wearing her unicorn pajamas, with the rainbow unicorn horn, and asked her "Isn't the unicorn horn still protecting us?" Vivian smiled.

Dad hung his head, "I am sorry to inform you," pausing, their Dad started to fake cry. Vivian went over to her Dad and held his large hand. "Go ahead Dad, whatever it is, it will be okay." In support, Valerie came over to the other side of their Dad and hugged him. Valerie proudly told him, whatever it is, we can handle it, Ohana, we are family and we are in this together!"

Proud of his mature daughters, their Dad wiped his fake tear away. "The news is Vivian, one of the pizzas is a veggie pizza, with peppers onions and broccoli, just the way you like it. Valerie, there's another pizza with pepperoni and pineapple, just the way you like it!" The girls sighed and smiled. Simultaneously, they both said, "thank you Mom and Dad!"

Mom continued, "And.......... You girls can eat it up in your room!" Screaming with delight the girls gave Mom and Dad each a huge hug, Then Vivian grabbed her pizza with the napkins, plates and forks and ran upstairs saying "You are the best Mom and Dad!" Valerie followed closely behind grabbing her pizza box with two cups and a two-liter bottle of Orange Crush, their absolute favorite. "Have fun!" Mom lovingly commanded.

The two sisters gracefully paraded up the stairs carrying their gourmet meals. "I thought you were kidding about the power of the rainbow unicorn horn, but boy, the power and the protection, it's almost unbelievable." Valerie commented. The younger, but very wise Vivian reminded Valerie "Believing is seeing, seeing is believing!" Stunned by her sister's wisdom, Valerie was speechless.

Valerie knew that the room was still a mess and wondered how they could make this castle idea really work. Before entering the room and reading her sister's mind, Vivian told her sister, "we tried, let's just enjoy the pizza and enjoy each other's company, that's what counts remember?" Knowing she had disappointed her sister Valerie hung her head in a moment of sadness.

Perfectly balancing the veggie pizza, Vivian grabbed the door handle to their bedroom. She opened the door slowly giving it another bump with her tiny hips. Scared because the lights were out, Vivian let Valerie go ahead of her with her pepperoni and pineapple pizza and the very heavy bottle of Orange Crush.

Walking backwards into their bedroom, Valerie walked blindly over to the oversized antique desk and put down the Orange Crush and her pizza box from Mod. Knowing Vivian was struggling with her pizza box, she quickly ran back to the doorway to help her sister. Vivian ran over to turn on the light, Valerie turned around trying to figure out what to do next.

Dad is the Best

As Vivian turned on the light, Valerie turned around and together they were shocked at what they saw. Looking around the room, Vivian was shocked, Valerie was amazed, Vivian was impressed, Valerie was in awe. Together they looked each other and started to scream, OMG, OMG! Smiling, jumping, and screaming the girls were ecstatic.

Hearing their precious girls scream with sounds of joy made Mom and Dad smile. As the girls continued to scream, Mom looked at Dad and asked, "What did you do up there?" Not waiting for an answer, Mom reached over to Dad and kissed him sweetly on his cheek. "The girls are lucky to have a father like you." Mom whispered in his ear. Dad sweetly replied, "I think you are wrong, I am lucky to have daughters like Valerie and Vivian, truly gifts from heaven."

The girls screaming continued for what seemed an eternity, Finally, screamed out, Valerie looked around. "Look, look at the castle walls, they're up and they look so good, just like Dad used to make. The tv with the DVD player is perfectly in place inside the castle and look, the DVDs for Beauty and the Beast, Lilo and Stitch and Cinderella are there. Almost in tears, Valerie noticed there was a basket full of art supplies with a note on it that said, "Follow your dreams." "Who could have done this?" she wondered.

Following her sister, Vivian stopped screaming and looked around the bedroom. Mr. Froggy was resting comfortably by her pillows, Booboo the Bear's arm was healed, and Willie the Whale was back in his aquarium, happy as a clam. The board games the girls used to play Chutes and Ladders, Connect Four and Candyland where all stacked neatly next to the temporary castle. And next to Valerie's huge basket of painting art supplies, stood an equally huge basket of drawing supplies marked Vivian. Valerie asked again, "Who could have done this?"

Putting her small arm around her sister and shaking her head Vivian looked at her sister and sarcastically asked "Really?". Valerie was confused, bewildered and mystified. Guessing wildly, she asked "Was it Santa Claus? Could of it been the Easter Bunny?" Pausing to think, Valerie continued "Maybe it was Cupid? Possibly Tom the Turkey? Oh, I know it was Mr. Dulany!"

Frustrated by her sister's answers, Vivian proudly gave her the answer. "Obviously, it had to be the power of the Unicorn's rainbow horn! Nobody else, nothing else could have done this. Not superman, not the Incredible Hulk, not the Guardians of the Galaxy!" Vivian said with conviction. "It was the power of the unicorn's rainbow horn!"

Downstairs Mom and Dad enjoyed their sausage, cheese green peppers, and onion deep-dish pizza from Giordano's as they watched the newest National Geographic special titled The Deep Blue Ocean, how much do we really Know? While they ate their deep-dish pizza, Mom and Dad thought about how proud they were of their daughters handling of the Covid-19 pandemic.

Upstairs, the girls started the party. Vivian grabbed her veggie pizza and a large glass of Orange Crush. As Valerie grabbed her pepperoni and pineapple pizza, Vivian asked Valerie what movie they should start with. Knowing they both needed a heavy dose of family, Valerie picked Lilo and Stich. Vivian picked Candyland as the game of choice.

Together the two had a blast together. They ate together They talked together. They watched movies together. They played board games together. They listened to Mexican music together. They danced the Renegade together. The important thing is they bonded together.

As they watched the third movie of the night Beauty and the Beast. Vivian imitated Belle when she was yelling at the Beast. "Control your temper!" Vivian said in a deep voice. Valerie smelled it first, then Vivian jumped up while playing Connect 4. Vivian said, "Could it be?" Valerie inhaled, exhaled and inhaled once again. Confidently she spoke, "I am positive, Mom has baked her world-famous chocolate chip cookies!"

Without wasting a single second Vivian and Valerie ran toward the door. Together they ran through the door. Together they ran down the stairs. Together they ran to the kitchen. Together they saw the big plate of Mom's world-famous chocolate cookies. Together they hugged their Mom and told her together that today was....... THE BEST DAY EVER!

Part Two

2

VALERIE AND THE BEANSTALK

Navy Beans

"Valerie, breakfast is ready. Its nine o'clock in the morning. This is the third time I have called you. Please come down now!" Valerie's mother strongly urged. Vivian, Valerie's younger sister, was politely listening to her mother's Mexican music in the background while she sat at the family dining room table eating her Kellogg's Frosted Flakes.

Half-asleep with sand still in her eyes, Valerie strolled in the kitchen still wearing her koala pajamas. Before saying a word, Valerie let out a huge yawn. Frustrated with her daughter, her mom commented "Nice..." but was quickly and rudely interrupted by Valerie asking, "What's for breakfast?"

Together Vivian and her mom both simultaneously said, "How rude?" They looked at each other and laughed. Then they both sniffed the air. Coughing, almost choking, together they asked, "What is that pungent odor?" Knowing it was neither of them, they stared at Valerie with disappointment.

Valerie did not care. She knew it was the pungent odor of stale hope. This quarantine was lasting too long. Valerie was staying home, except for walking their Beagle Chihuahua dog Kiara, three times a day, and helping her neighbor, Mr. Dulany with his garden. Valerie was tired of washing her hands constantly for twenty seconds and then sanitizing. Valerie was tired of doing her e-learning on the laptop. Valerie was tired of staying home. Valerie was tired of this whole Covid-19 situation.

"Valerie, why can't you be more like your sister Vivian?" asked a concerned Mom. "Vivian was up early this morning. She has showered, changed clothes took Kiara for a walk and came down for breakfast the first time I called." Valerie just sneered at her over-achieving younger sister.

Pausing for a second, her mother asked, "Aren't you going to eat?" Sitting their despondent, Valerie did not move. Seeing her sweet daughter was waiting for service, Mom sarcastically changed roles. Turning around as a waitress, she sweetly welcomed her guest, "Welcome to the V&V Diner!"

Continuing her charade, Valerie's Mom sarcastically asked "Would you like to see a menu? Or do you know what you would like?" Finally, things were looking up for Valerie. Smiling and taking Mom very seriously., Valerie decided to order, "Today I would like to start with a cup of hot chocolate, not too hot, gently stirred with exactly 18 mini-marshmallows. For breakfast, I would love to order a sausage and cheddar cheese omelet with chopped onions and crispy diced green peppers, served with golden brown hash browns and lightly toasted white bread, with a side of grape jelly. I will butter it myself." Valerie's Mom quietly turned around and went into the kitchen. "Please, do not forget the grape jelly" reminded Valerie.

Valerie was famished, with things looking up, maybe today she would shower and do her laundry. Maybe today she would take Kiara for a walk. Maybe today she would not die of boredom, maybe, maybe, maybe. After a few short minutes, the waitress, her mom returned carrying a small tray. Surprised with the hospitality, Valerie smiled and gratefully said "That was quick! Service here is excellent!" Sarcastically Valerie said, "Remind me to leave a good tip."

As Valerie sat there staring at her "awesome" sister Vivian, the waitress, served her special breakfast. Quickly noticing what was on the tray, she quickly became aggravated with the waitresses' flagrant error, Valerie rudely exclaimed "I didn't order Kellogg's Frosted Flakes with a glass of Tropicana orange juice with pulp!" Valerie paused as she pushed the small bowl of sugary flakes away. Without thinking, Valerie ordered the waitress to take the cereal back to the kitchen and bring the order she placed. Valerie crisscrossed her arms as a sign of disapproval.

Infuriated with her daughter's rudeness, but staying calm, her mom took a deep breath. Composing herself enough to reprimand her arrogant daughter, Mom cleared her throat, "Valerie, this is not a restaurant, you eat what is given to you. You need to appreciate what we have many families don't have breakfast."

"When is this going to end?" screamed a very frustrated Valerie. "I miss school, I miss going shopping, I miss my friends. I want to get my nails done and go shopping". Still smelling her rancid sister, Vivian finally looked up from her third-grade math book and sarcastically proclaimed "I agree, when is this smell going to stop, when are you going to wash those pajamas. Are you sure a koala really didn't die in your pajamas?"

"Valerie, currently there are plans to slowly open more stores back up, but right now, people are still getting sick from Covid-19. Many stores like Target and Menards are requiring everybody, shoppers, and employees, to wear face masks. Other stores like Walmart and Sam's Club are limiting the number of shoppers in their stores. There is no vaccine or a cure for Covid-19, for now, but there are many companies, as well as colleges working on the problem. For now, we still need to stay home and away from people" stated their mom.

"Please girls, finish your breakfast, cleanup and start your homework. Valerie, please, I beg you, take a shower before starting your homework," requested a very tired Mom. Vivian quickly replied, "yes Ma'am" and promptly rinsed her Tony the Tiger bowl and glass set and put them directly into their Whirlpool dishwasher. Valerie just sat there and stared into the small white bowl of soggy frosted flakes. "Valerie, wake-up!" shouted her mother.

As Vivian went upstairs, she unexpectedly turned around said "Thank you for breakfast Mom, Love you!" Their Mom smiled and quickly replied "Love you too!" Valerie sat at the kitchen table sulking, mad at the world, mad at her sister, mad at Mom. She quietly asked herself "What else can go wrong today?"

Watching her oldest daughter just sit in a pool of despair, did not make her mom happy. She knew her sweet daughter was drowning and needed to throw her a life preserver. Making sure Vivian was upstairs, her mom lovingly strolled over to Valerie and gave her a gentle hug telling her "I know this is tough, but we are your family, and we are in this together!" Unable to control the terrible stench of rotten eggs, expired milk and sweaty gym socks coming from Valerie's koala pajamas, Mom exclaimed "Girl, Vivian is right! After your shower, wash these! No soak them in Tide for three days and if doesn't work we will bury them!"

Already tired and emotionally unstable, Valerie's volcanic crater was building with gas, the pressure intensified with the last comment. With every ounce of self-control in her tiny body, Valerie tried to control the attitude from erupting from the volcano, but Valerie failed. Without warning, Mt. Valerie exploded, the volcano erupted, spreading hot attitude all over the house. Mt. Valerie was small but the attitude spewing from its peak was devasting.

"Vivian is right! Why can't you be more like your sister Vivian? Vivian walked the dog, Vivian did her homework, Vivian showered!" Continuing the devastation, Valerie remembered last night's fiasco. We watched a National Geographic special on Dolphins, I wanted to watch Animal Planet's show on abused animals, but no Vivian got to watch her show. We ordered pizza for the first time in a month, and you ordered a veggie pizza and the pepperoni and pineapple pizza I wanted, but what Vivian wanted. Vivian! Vivian! Vivian! Finally finished ranting, Valerie ran to the bathroom crying hysterically.

Cannellini Beans

The house was eerily quiet. Valerie's outburst was inappropriate, but understandable. The girl's mom and Dad were doing the best they knew how. This Covid-19 pandemic was new to everybody. Being in quarantine, not seeing friends, teachers, and family was not easy, not for Mom, Dad, Vivian, or Valerie. Everyone handled it their own way. Maybe a nice hot shower and a change of clothes would relax Valerie.

Valerie turned on the hot water and jumped in the shower. Soon, the small Princess bathroom was filled with steam from the scolding hot water. This is when her sweet mother snuck in. Worried about her eldest daughter, but loving her enough to give her space, Mom thought of a plan. First, she very carefully and quietly left two warm large blue bath towels on the vanity, next to Valerie's green cotton bathrobe, second, she cautiously kidnapped the offensive smelling koala pajamas from the floor.

Valerie startled her mom when she started to hum some Latin music that her mom never heard of, she thought to herself, "These kids and their music". As the room continued to fill with steam, Mom had one final mission. As Valerie showered, Mom calmly walked over to the steam covered mirror and with her finger sweetly wrote a message. Not wanting to interrupt her daughter she slyly left. The message simply wrote I LOVE YOU!!!

Finally running out of hot water, Valerie turned off the shower. Even with the TRESemme shampoo running low, Valerie was able to wash her gorgeous black hair three times getting rid of any rotten egg odors. She used a Lavender Dove body wash to remove any leftover Koala debris. Feeling much better and calmer she came out of the shower.

Quickly grabbing one of the blue bath towels Valerie dried herself off. With a slight chill in the morning air, she grabbed the green bathrobe and swiftly dressed herself. Realizing she was wearing her younger, smaller sister's robe she felt embarrassed to walk out of the room.

Being self-absorbed in her own pity, she never realized the special effort that her mom went through. Usually, Valerie appreciated what her parents did for her, but with this quarantine Valerie had changed. As she sank deeper in despair, Valerie started to forget everything her mom and Dad did for her and Vivian. Valerie also started to forget the sacrifices that her mom and Dad made for the small family. Valerie did not notice the fresh warm towels, the removal of the "dead" koala pajamas and when she opened the door, letting fresh air in, she never saw the message.

Being incredibly shy, Valerie opened the bathroom door that led into the bedroom she shared with Vivian. In the very small green bathrobe Valerie saw Vivian reading "The Unicorn Bandits", a story by Mr. Dulany. Almost whispering, Valerie calmly asked Vivian, "Would you please get my red shorts and red Hallsberry School Husky t-shirt in the third drawer of my dresser? The outfit is on the left-hand side, it is two outfits down."

Vivian just ignored her sister. Vivian did not look up from her book. Vivian did not say a word. Raising her voice, Valerie called "Vivian!" Vivian continued to ignore Valerie. Realizing nothing had changed, Valerie raised her voice again, "VIVIAN!" she screamed.

Afraid of Mt. Valerie exploding again, Vivian finally acknowledged Valerie. Frustrated with her sister's behavior, Vivian finally stood up, "Okay, okay, relax, red outfit third drawer on the left." Vivian quickly strolled over to the dresser and opened the third drawer. She opened the drawer, briefly glanced into the drawer, and suddenly closed the dresser drawer. Confidently, Vivian replied "Sorry, I don't see it!"

This was typical behavior for Vivian. A few weeks ago, Valerie was finishing a five-page report on the Westward expansion of early America. It included the California Gold Rush, The Louisiana Purchase, The Trail of Tears, The Mexican-American War and The Lewis and Clark Expedition, Valerie thought it was some of her best work. Mrs. Marino was very proud of her. After Valerie finished printing illustrations for the report, she asked Vivian to get the brown stapler from the kitchen drawer. Vivian opened the drawer, picked up a couple of no.2 pencils and said she could not find the stapler. Valerie had to get it herself.

Last week when they were helping their neighbor, Mr. Dulany with his preparations for getting his garden ready, she did the same thing. The soil needed to be turned over, cleaned, and prepared for future planting. Valerie was busy helping Mr. Dulany clean the massive garden when they came upon a massive unwanted dandelion. Valerie asked Vivian to go to the shed and get the shovel. Vivian opened the big grey barnyard doors of the shed, looked for ten seconds, and loudly banged the barnyard door shut. Vivian claimed she could not find the shovel. Valerie had to get it herself.

Having no choice, Valerie came out of the bathroom wearing the small green bathrobe. Laughing hysterically at her sister's choice of clothes, Vivian sarcastically asked her sister if she wanted to borrow anymore of her clothes. "You know, Mom and Dad will never let you leave this house dressed like that. Totally inappropriate, totally unacceptable, and totally punishable by grounding!" exclaimed a hilarious Vivian.

Humiliated by her younger sister, Valerie struggled with the bad day she was having. Valerie wondered what happened to the family that had her back, the family that stood beside her no matter what, and the family that loved her. Valerie quickly went over to the third drawer of her dresser, looked to the left under several outfits and grabbed the red shorts and the red Hallsberry Husky t-shirt that her sweet little sister could not find. Valerie had to get it herself. Valerie proceeded back to the bathroom to get dressed, in her clothes. The small house remained quiet the rest of the morning, except for an occasional bark of their beagle chihuahua mixed dog Kiara. Dad was busy working in his home office, Mom was busy cleaning the kitchen pantry. "I don't know why a buy all this food all the time. Canned vegetables, pasta, canned fruits, breakfast cereals, canned ravioli, and canned tuna. What am I going to do with all this food?" she asked herself. Making sure they were fresh, she put much of the extra food on the kitchen table.

Since this was Friday, May 1, 2020, the girls both knew they had to finish the assignments from their teachers at Hallsberry School. It was announced on Monday that going back to school this year was not going to happen, but the Hallsberry Huskies were expected to continue learning on their laptops. All morning, Vivian and Valerie worked relentlessly on their laptops. Vivian worked on her division, subtraction, addition, and multiplication. She worked on graphing and word problems. Vivian wondered why Amy had to share her 25 pieces of tootsie rolls with four friends. Obviously, any extra she would get to keep.

Vivian liked to read, she had just finished the first Harry Potter book, "Harry Potter and the Sorcerer's Stone." She was looking forward to the second installment in the series, "Harry Potter and the Chamber of Secrets." Being incredibly ambitious, her goal was to finish the whole series before the quarantine was over.

Valerie was concentrating on writing her story. Mrs. Marino had taught the class about developing characters, creating a plot line, inventing a problem, and finding a solution to the problem. Their story could be set in the past, present, or future. Their unique story must be a fantasy and could happen anywhere or any place. Valerie's story would be of a young girl who helped her neighbor plant his spring garden.

Suddenly Mom called "Lunch is ready! Come and get it!" Knowing the expectation, Vivian quickly put down "The Unicorn Bandit" and ran to help her mom. Not to be out done by her sister, Valerie also put down her "story" and ran down the stairs to help her mom. Very loudly the girls competed for their mom's attention and approval. Simultaneously, the girls eagerly shouted, "What can I do for you Mom?"

Instantly Mom shushed them, putting her finger over her lips. "Dad is on a conference call with a client!" whispered Mom. "We need to keep quiet!" In an indoor quiet voice Vivian asked how she could help. Happy her girls were willing to help Mom quietly answered, "Please set the table."

Vivian was very athletic and competitive. Taunting her older sister Vivian boasted "I can set the table better and faster than you!" Noticing the kitchen table was full of groceries Vivian asked her mother if they were eating in the dining room. Calling from his home office in a normal voice Dad unexpectantly answered "Yes! And please set a place for Dad"

Black Beans

Accepting her sister's table setting challenge, Valerie set the rules. "First one to completely set two complete place settings wins. Okay?" Vivian accepted the challenge. In anticipation of winning Valerie announced "GO!" Together the race begun.

Mom was busy cooking lunch, Dad was finishing his work, neither one noticed the incredible race for supremacy. Vivian grabbed her placemats, Valerie grabbed her forks, spoons and knives, Vivian brought her plates, Valerie brought her glasses. Running out of breath, both girls eyed each other, first one to bring, fold and place the napkins would be the champ. Vivian completed one napkin with Valerie close behind. Each sister had one napkin to go, Vivian was a millisecond ahead of Valerie when she dropped the napkin, Valerie now had the edge.

Competing for their dignity, the girls continued to battle. Vivian swiftly picked up her napkin. Seeing her sister begin to fold the final napkin made Vivian begin to sweat. Out of nowhere, Valerie got a papercut, giving Vivian the opportunity to catch up. Battling feverishly, the girls raced to place the final napkin. The girls continued to stare at each other, both raised their napkin ready to place it down as the pressure mounted, simultaneously they both slammed their napkins in place. It was a tie.

In a competition, sisters never settled for a tie, it was an unwritten law. Curious what was going on, Mom asked "What is going on in there?" Vivian promptly answered "Nothing?" Mom quickly replied, "Is anybody hurt, bleeding or crying?" Vivian replied again "NO!" Valerie answered, "The less you know the better!" Mom laughing said "I heard that!" and quickly went back to making lunch.

"We need to settle this!" demanded Valerie. "I got an idea!" suggested Vivian. "Hey Mom, what's for lunch?" she politely asked. "We are having my homemade tacos, with all the fixings, sour cream, crispy chopped lettuce, vine-ripened tomatoes, fresh guacamole and freshly sliced jalapeno peppers, complete with true homemade Mexican rice boasted Mom. "Excellent!" replied Dad. "How long before lunch? He asked, "I need time to wash and sanitize my hands."

"Five minutes at the most!" answered Mom. "Girls help me bring everything for the tacos to the table" requested Mom. "That's it!" exclaimed Valerie. "Whoever eats the most tacos at lunch wins!" she proudly stated. "That's stupid!" answered Vivian. "Last time we had an eating contest, remember with the chocolate chip cookies, we both were throwing up for days." "I say a lot of stupid things" proudly declared Valerie.

As Mom called the girls, Vivian had a brilliant idea. "Come on Vivian, come on Valerie, lunch is getting cold." Vivian quickly explained the game, "Whoever brings the most things to the table wins, big bowls are worth five points, medium ones three and small bowls are worth one point. Any questions?" Valerie shook her head. "Winner, take all!" Vivian started to run as she slyly announced "GO!"

"Doesn't she ever stop?" Valerie asked herself as she ran into the kitchen behind Vivian. Vivian grabbed the large pot of Mom's Mexican rice, followed closely behind with Valerie grabbing the medium pot of perfectly seasoned ground beef. The war was on, Vivian raced to take the crispy lettuce while Valerie took the ripe chopped tomatoes. On the way back to the kitchen Vivian tripped on Kiara, giving Valerie the opportunity to take the lead. Vivian complained, but Valerie arrogantly answered, "All is fair in love and war!" The war continued.

Valerie had a distinct lead as Vivian composed herself. Valerie paraded easily into the kitchen seizing the cheddar and chihuahua cheese bowls. Vivian trying to desperately catch up tried grabbing the hot salsa bowl and the medium salsa bowl, seeing her younger daughter juggle the two bowls, Mom told Vivian to take one bowl at a time. Returning quickly, Valerie offered to take the hot salsa and abruptly took the small bowl into the dining room, Valerie's lead was increasing.

The war continued with Valerie clearly winning. Vivian had to change her strategy however, the opportunities were diminishing. Mom did not realize what the girls were doing and called, "Come on Dad, the girls are almost done! I do not know what has gotten into them." Then an idea hit Vivian, but the timing had to be perfect.

Valerie grabbed the fresh corn tortillas and Vivian quickly followed taking the flour tortillas. All that was left was the large carton of Supremo sour cream and a freshly made bowl of Mom's fresh guacamole. Seizing the opportunity for the ultimate victory, Vivian raced to grab the sour cream and guacamole, however although the very athletic Vivian had a slight lead, Valerie "miraculously" managed to pass Vivian and steal the two remaining points. As she raced to put the remaining condiments on the table Valerie arrogantly looked back and stared at Vivian.

What she did not see was unfortunate. At the same time Valerie was racing towards the dining room table, Dad was concentrating on talking to his client on his cell phone. Neither one saw what was coming, two laws were being broken, no walking while on the phone and always look forward when you carry food. Mystifying, how two wrongs do not make a right.

No one knew how they escaped with no broken bones. It was like two freight trains speeding on a collision course for certain destruction. Two male Mountain Rams bucking their horns for the right to date a female ram. It was like two all-star fifth graders going for the soccer ball. All scenarios led to one thing, unthinkable damage, unthinkable pain, and this was like no other collision.

Vivian had timed this perfectly. Victory would belong to Vivian. It was like the Fourth of July fireworks, lots of noise and plenty of bang. Suddenly Dad yelled "NO!" and it happened, man against girl. The size of Dad literally knocked the tiny Valerie across the room causing the sour cream and guacamole to also fly straight into the air. First, the fresh green guacamole plopped down on Dad's clean white work shirt as he laid on the dining room floor. Next came the sour cream spreading awkwardly across his freshly ironed black dress work pants.

As Dad laid laughing at what happened he said, "Thank goodness none of landed on my head!" Then he laid back and bumped the dining room table leg. Down came the bowl of hot salsa on top of his head. "Are you okay dad?" asked a concerned Mom. "I think so, maybe a bit banged up, but I will be okay" chuckled Dad.

Vivian ran to get some towels to help Dad clean up the sour cream, salsa and guacamole that was spread across his body. Being a comedian Vivian told Dad, "You have the sour cream, salsa, and guacamole. All you need is the chips, and you are a walking nacho party!" Everyone laughed but Valerie.

While the rest of the family was having fun with the walking nacho party, Valerie was still lying motionless on the ground. Valerie announced her condition. "Hello, I was hurt too" she bashfully said. "Valerie, you need to be more careful!" scolded Mom, "You almost hurt Dad!" Very dramatically Valerie repeated "Hello, I'm hurt too." Mom quickly answered "Vivian, why don't you go take care of your sister while I take care of Dad."

Begrudgingly, Vivian went to take care of her older sister. Being compassionate, she checked and found no broken bones, just a broken ego. Whispering to Valerie, Vivian told Valerie that without the sour cream and guacamole, she lost the battle, if she would have successfully brought the condiments to the table she would have won. Valerie angrily whispered back "That's not fair, you cheated!" As Vivian helped her fallen comrade up from the ground, Vivian happily used the same exact words that her sister used previously, "All is fair in Love and War!"

4

Lima Beans

Mom did her best trying to reheat everything for lunch. However, for this taco lunch there would be no sour cream, no fresh guacamole, and no hot salsa. Mom did not need to say anything, the look of disappointment from her big brown eyes said everything. Dad quickly changed into some fresh clothes and returned to the dining room table. As he sat across from Valerie he started talking, "Valerie, I love you, but........", that's when Valerie stopped listening.

Like a cheetah sitting high up in a tree, she looked down on her empty plate, waiting to pounce. Her Dad finished talking ".... anymore." Not sure if she was paying attention, Dad asked "Are you paying attention?" Valerie looked at her dad and shook her head yes. Next Valerie looked at Vivian who was silently singing, I am the winner, I am the winner, no time for Valerie.

Saved by her mom's sudden appearance bringing back the reheated seasoned ground beef, Valerie took a deep breath. Then she pounced down on the taco lunch. She attacked the Mexican rice, she devoured the first two beef tacos piled high with shredded cheddar cheese, crispy chopped lettuce, and vine-ripened chopped tomatoes, topped with the less spicy medium salsa. She practically growled and showed her fangs when Vivian tried to steal her catch. There would be no scraps for the scavengers.

Mom and Dad were quiet. Although they loved the girls, it was exhausting being their chef, their teacher, their fitness instructor and their maid 24 hours a day, 7 days a week. Mom remained quiet while Dad started asking Mom if there was any news from Hallsberry School about the girls returning to finish the school year. Mom just sighed, hoping Dad would change the subject.

Except for the occasional "Please pass the....", it was extremely quiet. Vivian did not like quiet, although very shy, she liked talking and she loved the art of conversation. Vivian tried to start a conversation but did not know what to talk about. She thought of Mom, nothing came, she looked at Dad, he still looked mad. Then she looked at Valerie, she thought about how pretty she was, she thought about how smart she was, and Vivian thought about what a great sister Valerie was. Vivian hoped she grow up to be just like her sister. "No, nothing there to talk about" Vivian said to herself.

Still exploring the possibilities of conversation, Vivian quickly scanned the room. Vivian saw Kiara sleeping on the sofa, Mom would get upset. She saw the family portrait leaning against the wall, waiting to be hung, Dad would get upset. Finally, she saw the empty carton of sour cream laying on the floor. Smiling, she thought about the Dollop of Daisy commercial, then her senses quickly came back to her, Mt. Valerie would erupt, absolutely, positively, no Valerie.

Almost ready to give up Vivian exhaled. What would her volleyball team think, what would her soccer coach and neighbor think about Vivian giving up? Failure was not an option. She continued to scan the living room, then out of the corner of her eye, it hit her. Striking gold, she wasted no time in asking, "So Mom, why are those groceries out on the kitchen table?"

Mom was surprised that her sweet, shy, little daughter Vivian was the one to break the ice. Finishing her non sour cream, no guacamole, no hot salsa corn tortilla beef taco with chihuahua cheese Mom wiped her mouth with the special Signature select red, white, and blue napkins and smiled. "I thought you would never ask!" replied the proud Mom.

Dad said "thank you" to Mom for the special lunch and escorted himself back to his home office. Dad politely picked up his plate, fork and glass and brought to the kitchen sink on his way to the office. Mom continued, "I was cleaning the pantry this morning and I realized how fortunate we are. Every day we put food on our table, yet, every day, many families in this community cannot feed their children, they rely on food pantries. We do not need all this food. So tomorrow, I will pack this extra food and take it to the food pantry.

Worried, Valerie cautiously begged "You're not donating our toilet paper, are you?" Anxious about her mom's desire to help the world, Valerie admitted "I can live without my Peach Iced Tea, I can live without my cell phone, and I can live without my TRESemme shampoo, but I cannot live without my Charmin bath tissue!" Vivian laughed and teased her sister "Charity begins in the Bathroom!"

"Can I go with you to the food pantry?" pleaded Vivian. As Mom and the girls started to clean the lunch dishes, Mom answered "Tomorrow I am going to drop this food at the food pantry and then stop by Target for some milk and eggs." The key word was Target. Vivian begged her mom to take her, "I really need some craft paint for my artwork!" Valerie wasted no time in requesting her desired item, "All I need is a new bottle of OPI white nail polish, I want to give myself a manicure and a pedicure! Mom just smiled and said, "We will see!"

Together they cleaned the dining room table. Together they loaded the dishwasher, as promised the leftovers were miniscule, a few strands of shredded lettuce, that was all. Together they packed the nonperishable grocery items. Together they put the boxes in the car.

Separately Mom went to watch General Hospital, her favorite soap opera. She loved watching the relationship between Sonny and Carly. Separately Vivian worked on her violin lessons. Her goal was to be first chair, string section, in the Glenbard Central High School orchestra with her best friend Evelyn. Separately Valerie went to work on her story. The goal was to start and finish the story, of a girl helping her neighbor in the garden, by the end of the day. Valerie had no ideas for the story.

Mom intently watched General Hospital. Sonny ran the mob in Port Charles, Carly ran a gourmet restaurant in Port Charles. Together they made it work and the future was promising. Like Evelyn, Vivian practiced her violin. Evelyn played the high notes, Vivian played the low notes. Together they made it work and the future was promising. Valerie started to write her story she opened her laptop. Kiara came to play. Together they did not write the story and the future was bleak.

Pinto Beans

Saturday Morning

Saturdays, the best day of the week. Saturday is the Mufasa of the lions. Saturday is the vanilla of the ice cream world, Saturday is the Portello's hot dog, all the best, all the crème of the crop. There was no school on Saturday, best day ever. They went shopping to Target on Saturday, best day ever. Mom made Eggo waffles for breakfast every Saturday, best day ever. As Valerie opened her big brown eyes, she stretched and yawned, thinking to herself, "Today will be a great day!"

Excited about today's prospects, Valerie hopped out of bed. She quickly brushed her teeth and brushed her long black hair. For twenty seconds she washed her hands and face. Wearing only an over-sized white t-shirt and shorts, Valerie changed into her Levi blue jeans, a simple but elegant white top with a yellow daisy on the left shoulder and her blue open toed sandals, all in preparation for Saturday's big day. Then Valerie's world changed forever.

Vivian's bed was made. Vivian was up and already downstairs. Like a stray deer running from a hungry fox, Valerie rushed down the stairs into the kitchen. Relieved, because there was no Vivian, Valerie decided to toot her own horn. "I am going to take Kiara out for a quick walk, okay Mom?" proudly asked Valerie.

Smiling proudly Mom started to say something but was quickly interrupted by Valerie. "Isn't nice to have an ambitious daughter?" Finally, Mom started to talk, "Yes, it is. Vivian has been up for hours, Vivian helped pack the rest of the extra groceries in the car, Vivian helped me set the table for breakfast, Vivian had her breakfast. Vivian cleaned her dishes and took Kiara for a walk. Vivian should be back soon. Valerie angrily thought to herself "Vivian, Vivian, Vivian!" but said to her mother, "What a great sister!"

Excited to be home, Kiara started to bark. Valerie commanded Kiara to stop barking, Kiara continued barking. Vivian commanded Kiara to stop barking, Kiara stopped. Frustrated, Valerie sat down for breakfast. Not wanting to replay the waitress game Valerie patiently waited for her favorite Eggo waffles. In anticipation she tightly held the bottle of Vermont maple syrup, salivating, she watched as Mom turned around.

As Mom slowly walked over to Valerie, the anticipation grew. She had waited all week for the piece de resistance of the breakfast world, Eggo waffles smothered in butter and fresh maple syrup. It did not matter that Vivian was decked out in an all-white shoulderless sundress with her brunette hair brushed back into a ponytail. It did not matter that Vivian woke up earlier than her and impressed Mom by taking Kiara for a five-mile walk. It did matter that mom was serving Eggo waffles.

The anticipation was overwhelming, this only happened once a week. Biting her nails, she started to sweat as her mom approached. She closed her eyes as she thanked God for the tasty-toasted treats. Then it happened, the impossible, the incident, the mistake. Mom put down a bowl of Kellogg's Raisin Bran. Mystified, Valerie bit her lip as she calmly asked, "What happened to MY Eggo waffles?"

Vivian quickly answered, "I'm sorry Valerie, I woke up early this morning, helped Mom finish packing the groceries in the car and that five mile walk with Kiara, well it, it really built up an appetite, I was hungry,

I must have finished them." Disappointed, Valerie just stared at Vivian. Vivian sensed that Mt. Valerie was ready to explode. Terrified, she hollered "Mom!"

Calming herself, Valerie took a deep breath, and another deep breath, she still had no homework, and she was still going to Target. Two out of Three still can make this an awesome Saturday. Defeated with breakfast, Valerie picked the raisins out of the Raisin Bran and choked down the Bran. Vivian witnessed Valerie's reaction to the bran and shot the imaginary arrow. Vivian silently sung the words, "I am the winner, I am the winner, no time for Valerie." The war was back on.

Frustrated with her over-achieving sister, Valerie decided it was time to shoot an imaginary arrow of her own. Using Mom as a hostage, Valerie asked "When are we leaving for the food pantry? I have some more money I have upstairs I would like to give to the food pantry." "That's very nice! Replied Mom.

Knowing Mom only had plans to drop off the food, Valerie shot another imaginary arrow solely to impress Mom. "Can we stay all day? Maybe we can help pass out the food to those less fortunate." With a tear in her eye, Mom was crushed with her daughter's empathy, the arrow had worked. Not ready to concede, Vivian fired a missile, "With social distancing and occupancy limits we will never be allowed in the building."

"It's the thought that counts!" Mom said as she defended Valerie. Encouraged, Valerie felt she was finally winning the war. Trying to deflect the emergency support from reaching Valerie's base, Vivian decided to change battlefields. Quickly deflecting Valerie's advancement, Vivian asked, "Are we still going to Target today?"

Shocked at the long pause from Mom, both girls were mystified. This long pause was not part of the war strategy. This was Saturday, this is Target Day, this was tradition. Hesitantly, Mom began to speak. "With this pandemic happening, Dad feels you girls should stay home. He thinks you won't follow the social distancing rule, which is of course six feet, and he feels you won't keep your face masks on, which is now mandatory."

The enemy had now changed, Valerie and Vivian did not see this coming. They would have to unite to battle the new enemy, Mom. Vivian started shooting reasons why they should go first, "We are smart, we do well in school, we keep our room clean, we eat our vegetables, we brush our teeth, and we do our chores", exhausted, she finally ran out of ammunition.

Knowing that Mom was a strong unbeatable force, Valerie started shooting larger rounds of reasons. Being an experienced soldier, Valerie brought out the big reason why they should go, "Mom, Saturday at Target is tradition, like putting up a Christmas tree every year, like taking you to brunch at La Campana, every Mother's Day. Tradition like dressing up for Easter Sunday, tradition like balloons for our birthday. Throwing the most powerful weapon, the guilt grenade, Valerie said "you wouldn't stop any of these traditions, why would you stop our Saturday tradition at Target?"

Unexpectantly, Mom laughed. "I'm sorry girls, this is not my decision. It was Dad's and I will not go against his orders, the battle is with him, not me." Shocked at the blast of information, the girls were stunned, powerless to move or speak. Quickly recovering from the blast of information, the girls looked at each other trying to figure out a new battle plan.

"However," Mom reluctantly replied, "This General needs supplies for the base, we need to leave in five minutes. I really want no girl left behind, but I will not go against Commander Dad." Then the explosion went off inside Valerie's head, "We will attack him from the north and from the south, he won't know what hit him." Valerie announced. Ready to fight, the girls marched towards Dad's camp, his home office.

Before surprising Dad with their ambush, the girls planned their strategy. Armed with adorable smiles they simultaneously broke the perimeter of the General's quarters. Then they threw the first in their arsenal, "Morning Daddy" they both sweetly said. Dad was unprepared, melting and losing his backbone Dad started to talk, but the girls went in for the unthinkable, a move usually saved for the more experienced green berets or the elite Marines.

Dad was mystified, he tried to fight off his daughters. When his daughters were younger, General Dad was unprepared for daughters, they cried, they got what they wanted. They eventually learned all they had to do was smile and show their big brown eyes and the battle was won. General Mom taught General Dad to give only his name, rank, and serial number. He kept repeating Dad, General, 3847, Dad, General, 3847, Dad, General, 3847.

The move is now known in the family as the V&V hug. Powerful and dangerous, avoid it at all costs, however Dad was cornered, there was no way out. Preparing for the worse Dad tried to activate his force field, it was too late, Dad was powerless. The girls were relentless, the girls were unsympathetic, the girls were merciless as they synchronized hugging their dad. With Dad, it was hopeless, he had no chance for survival.

The most powerful weapon known to man, the V&V hug took down Dad in record time. With no backbone left, Vivian and Valerie felt now what the time to strike, Valerie courteously let Vivian interrogate him first. Stepping back, but close enough to hold his large hand, Vivian started her deceptive strategy. In a sweet quiet voice Vivian began, "Daddy, I love you soo very, very much, Mommy says I can't go to Target to get paint unless you say it's okay." Emptying the arsenal of weapons, Vivian dug deep and gave her dad the pouty lips and the batting eyes look.

Totally beaten by Vivian, General Dad surrendered. "You have been a good girl, you have done your homework and helped around the house, your strategy has worked. Please wear a face mask and keep six feet apart from other shoppers. You my precious Vivian, may go with your mom to Target. Besides, I can never say no to my Vivian" Ecstatic and overwhelmed with her victory, Vivian gave her dad a special hug and ran off the battlefield to be with Mom.

Valerie was stunned, was beating Dad that easy? Sensing it was Valerie decided to put it all on the line and take down General Dad swiftly and quietly. Putting Dad out of his misery was the kind thing to do. Valerie boldly asked Dad, "Can I go to Target, I really need some OPI white nail polish?" Dad said nothing. Not to be done by her younger sister, Valerie went in for the final blow "Daddy, I love you sooo much!" followed by the batting eyes and pouty lips.

Dad said nothing. Valerie started to celebrate her victory. Dad surrendered to Vivian he would certainly surrender to her. Then Dad ambushed her, quickly turning the war around, Dad fired back with bombs of negativity, "You have NOT been a good girl, you have NOT done your homework and you have NOT helped around the house. Your strategy has NOT worked. You may NOT go to Target with Mom and Vivian. You Will go to your room and finish your story about a girl helping her neighbor."

Vivian was shocked. Mom was mystified. Valerie was mortally wounded. Where did this dad come from? Embarrassed, she lost the war, Valerie succumbed to her emotions. Mt. Valerie began to erupt. First, you take away my Eggo waffles on a Saturday. Then you take away my trip to Target on a Saturday and then you tell me to do homework on a Saturday! On top of it you let Vivian go to Target! Vivian! Vivian! Vivian! Worst sister ever! Worst Mom ever! Worst Dad ever!"

As Mt Valerie continue to erupt rivers of hot attitude, Valerie cried hysterically. Mom failed as she tried to comfort her daughter. Dad failed as he tried to comfort his daughter. Vivian failed as she tried to comfort her sister. "You do not have my back! This is the worse family ever!" Mad as a hornet, Valerie cried "I wish you were never my family." Like a F5 tornado, Valerie stormed out of the room headed straight to her bed to privately cry. Valerie continued crying until she fell into a deep sleep.

Gravy Beans

Sleeping for what seemed hours, Valerie started to wake up. With sand still in her eyes and bitterness running rampant in her heart, Valerie deliberately pulled the big pink Cinderella comforter cover back over her head. She tossed, she turned, she laid on her right side, then her left, she attempted to lay on her back, and finally Valerie tried to lay on her stomach.

Relentlessly, she tried falling back to sleep, but the anger running through her mind was too much. Like a broken record, her bright young mind kept repeating "No Eggo waffles today, No Valerie today, No Target today, No Valerie today, No homework free day today, No Valerie." Over-and-over again, her mind repeated those hideous words. Unable to stop it, unable to tolerate it anymore, she laid in her bed, still under her covers and screamed at the top of her lungs "Please stop!"

Valerie woke up hungry. She immediately thought of all the kids at Hallsberry School who had nothing to eat. There was a pain in her gut, and she wondered how they managed to live without eating. Barely touching the Kellogg's Raisin Bran, her stomach began growling. The growling would not stop, it was becoming unbearable. Having watched too many Disney Princess movies, Valerie knew there was only one way to fix the hunger problem, make a wish. That is exactly what she did.

VALERIE AND THE BEANSTALK

"I wish, I wish to solve the hunger problem in my stomach and my unknown hungry friends at Hallsberry School" Valerie said as she didn't know the official protocol of wishing, was she supposed to click her heels? Was she supposed to say, bippety boppety boo? She did not know, but she knew she had to get out of bed.

As she forcibly took herself out of bed, she noticed two things. First, nobody came running, all this talk about having my back, all this talk about family helping family was just that, talk. Second, on her nightstand next to her bed was a large stack of freshly toasted Eggo waffles, topped with a melting slab of creamy butter and smothered, yes smothered in fresh hot Vermont maple syrup. The steam was still coming from the waffles.

Thankful the plate was there Valerie did not think twice. Not wanting to be ungrateful to the chef, Valerie quickly devoured the large stack of Eggo Waffles. Thirsty, she grabbed the tall glass of orange juice and washed down the delicious waffles. As she drank the tall glass of sunshine, she noticed it was pulp free, just the way Valerie liked it, not with pulp like Vivian liked it. Things were finally looking up.

Thinking her family had changed, Valerie was excited. Mom, Dad and Vivian were probably downstairs waiting to apologize. Valerie wished Mom and Dad were going to be holding a giant banner declaring their apology. Vivian wished they would be holding a dozen helium balloons, two light blue, two emerald green, two rose red, two royal purple, two bright yellow together with one shiny silver balloon indicating that their daughter was #1.

Mom loved taking pictures. She took pictures of everything. Mom took pictures of the first time Valerie walked, the first time Valerie drank milk, the first time Valerie played soccer, the first time she ate broccoli, Mom would certainly take pictures of them apologizing for their rude behavior. Valerie had to change out of her wrinkled clothes, quickly, she was not going to miss the "surprise" party.

Ultimately, Valerie chose her mustard yellow sundress. It was simple but elegant, perfect for the party and perfect for pictures. Paired with her yellow sandals and a sunflower barrette pulling her stylish black hair away from her beautiful face. Valerie was ready for her grand entrance.

Walking slowly down the staircase, Valerie, prepared herself for the "surprise". As she came to the last stair she held on to the banister, she could not afford to have Mom take another disastrous picture on Facebook. The humiliation, the shame, the relentless bullying from her friends at school, Mom needed to be more careful what she put on Facebook.

As she looked in the kitchen, Valerie thought about all the bad moments Mom posted on Facebook. Potty training, falling off her bike, the measles, the time she got food poisoning, drooling while she slept, the embarrassing list went on and on. Valerie thought there should be a law with Mom and cameras. Valerie continued searching the house for her "surprise" party.

Having found nothing in the kitchen Valerie entered the dining room, no party. Then the living room, nothing, then the downstairs bathroom, nothing (Thank goodness). Discouraged, but hopeful, Valerie worked her way down the rickety stairs to the dark, cold basement, no party. Valerie checked Dad's office, still nothing but a brochure on the Philippines. Valerie wished she could go to the Philippines.

Maybe it was upstairs in her parent's room, she hurried to the last unchecked room in the house. After straightening her pretty-mustard yellow dress and hand brushing her hair she quickly opened the door and jumped in, but there was no party.

Disgusted at the thought of her family abandoning her, Valerie decided to make some more wishes. The first wish would be an unlimited shopping spree at Target, and she wished to have a Subaru sedan, just like Dad's." Taking a moment to think, Valerie also wished for lunch later from

Panda Express and in complete bitterness, she also repeated her wish to never see her family again.

Laughing and back to reality, Valerie thought the celebration might be outside. "It's a beautiful day outside, no clouds, no rain, 70 degrees, perfect for my apology celebration," she said to herself as she frantically raced to the back door. Attempting to give her mom the perfect photo Valerie smiled as she headed outside. The bright sun quickly blinded her. She quickly put her hand over eyes, not seeing Kiara, she tripped and fell, screaming "Help!"

Mr. Dulany, her neighbor, came running. Valerie and Mr. Dulany had been friends for years and helping her was like helping one of his children. As this was May, Mr. Dulany spent many hours outside preparing his massive garden for planting. Since early April he had planted seeds inside, waiting for the right time to transfer them outside.

Planting a huge garden was no easy task. Years ago, Mr. Dulany had bad luck with gardens, but he figured out it was not his lack of a green thumb, it was the soil. Instead of rich, black loose soil, where roots could grow freely and vegetable plants could produce abundantly, Glendale Heights was cursed with heavy spots of clay soil. Brownish thick, poorly nourished, clay where roots are cramped and enslaved to the clay, where vegetable and flower plants would be stunted and grow very little, if any.

Knowing the problem and being an optimist, Mr. Dulany knew there was an answer, but where it was, what it was, was elusive. Thinking outside the box, Mr. Dulany eventually came up with his "Bucket Farm". Each plant would get their own five-gallon bucket filled with rich black dirt and the ability to grow unconditionally on their own. For drainage, he drilled three holes in the side of each five-gallon bucket.

However, every Spring as the years went by, not only was Mr. Dulany getting older, but his "Bucket Farm" was getting larger. Although Valerie did not like dirt, let alone getting dirty, she loved working the garden with

Mr. Dulany. He was a kind, patient man who listened to her and taught her about gardening. Valerie loved watching the garden grow, it was mystifying how with a little water and a little love the plants prospered and produced an assortment of vegetables.

Mr. Dulany planted his garden in different phases. A little in April, a little in May and a little in June, this way he did not have an over- abundant harvest in August. Valerie enjoyed watching and being part of something bigger, the tomatoes, the peppers, the broccoli, the beans, the cucumbers, the onions, the potatoes, and the herbs. Valerie loved how Mr. Dulany shared his harvest with everybody, the teachers at Hallsberry School, the neighbors and especially her family.

Azuki Beans

Hearing the frantic scream of a young girl, yelling "Help!" Mr. Dulany looked up from his freshly rearranged buckets and saw Valerie laying on the ground. Without hesitation, Mr. Dulany quickly sprang into action. Putting down his small shovel, throwing off his blue garden gloves, he raced around the fence to help his good neighbor Valerie.

Within seconds he was there. Mr. Dulany was helping Valerie get up. Worried, but seeing nothing physically wrong with her, Mr. Dulany carefully asked "Are you okay? Can you stand? What are you doing home alone?". Valerie just sulked. Mr. Dulany quickly retrieved one of the brown cushioned lawn chairs that was on her back patio. "Sit down, do you want me to call 911? Do you want me to call your parents?"

Realizing that there was no surprise party or apology party, Valerie just sat there drowning in her sea of despair. Not knowing what was wrong with Valerie, Mr. Dulany said "I will call your mom and call 911." Realizing he did not have a phone, rarely did ever carry it, he anxiously said he was going back to his house to call for help."

Suddenly, Helen Keller began to talk, it was a miracle. Valerie pleaded with Mr. Dulany, "please do not leave me, I am fine." Realizing all she had was a bruised ego, Mr. Dulany asked why she was home alone, it was not like her mom and Dad to leave Valerie home alone.

All the kids at Hallsberry School knew they could talk to Mr. Dulany, in confidence. He would listen and try to help, he would not judge, and he would not gossip. Valerie felt fortunate to live next door to such a wonderful adult. Mr. Dulany was the kind of adult that built you up, never competing with you, just supporting everything you did. She thought about the time when Jose' was bullying her in second grade, she went to Mr. Dulany on the playground. He talked to Jose' immediately and the bullying stopped, instantly and forever.

Mr. Dulany was different than other adults, some say he had a rough childhood, others say he loved the kids so much, it changed his heart. Either way he liked to use comedy in his relationships. He teased both Valerie and Vivian constantly, but they knew Mr. Dulany loved them. Thinking Mr. Dulany was using comedy, He started to speak, "Did you hear ten, yes ten semi-trailers full of food pulled up to Hallsberry School this morning?" Valerie waited for the punch line. "The head driver handed Principal Aaliyah a note, all it said was Enjoy, compliments of Valerie." Valerie was speechless.

"Come on, let's go over to my patio. I will get some nice cold Lipton Peach Tea and we can tell you shouldn't be home alone." Holding her small hand, they walked silently to his patio. He asked Valerie to sit down and wait, just a minute or two and he would be back. When he was inside Mr. Dulany called her parents. As she patiently sat there, Valerie noticed how few plants were planted. Quickly, Mr. Dulany returned carrying two ice filled cold glasses of Lipton Peach Tea, he handed one to Valerie.

Valerie quickly took the sweaty glass from Mr. Dulany. Drinking it like she was an African Elephant who just crossed the Savannah Desert and found her first watering hole in days, Valerie put the glass down on the patio table, and wiped her mouth with her right arm. Not being shy with her neighbor, Mt. Valerie started to erupt, "Do you really want to know what's wrong?" Not waiting for an answer. Valerie said "No Eggo waffles on Saturday, No Target run on Saturday, and No homework free Saturday! It is always about Vivian!" starting to cry, Valerie sniffled out "And I got all dressed up or an apology party that never even existed!

Mr. Dulany was baffled, this was not a national emergency, this was Valerie overreacting to her parent's discipline. This was Valerie making a mountain out of a mole hill. This was Valerie. Trying to comfort her, Mr. Dulany held her as she cried her eyes out. Finally stopping the waterfall, Valerie asked "Can I stay with you until my parents get back?"

Happily, surprised at Valerie's request, and knowing her parents knew and trusted where she was, Mr. Dulany smiled and said "Sure, but what are we going to do?" Valerie liked volunteering at school, at church and with her neighbor Mr. Dulany. He was not in the best of health and based on what she has seen, he is behind in his planting. Smiling with enthusiasm Valerie proudly announced "We are going to plant today! Are you with me?" Looking at her mustard yellow sundress, Valerie told Mr. Dulany that she would be right back, "This outfit is for a party, I need an outfit for gardening"

Waiting and watching, Mr. Dulany patiently waited for Valerie. Mr. Dulany waited....... and waited....... and waited. Having a daughter of his own, Angelica, Mr. Dulany knew the importance of picking out the right outfit for the right occasion. Finally, Valerie emerged from her back door and ran around to Mr. Dulany's back yard excited somebody was paying attention to her.

Mr. Dulany smiled as she came running toward him. Remembering social distancing they gave each other a huge air high five and smiled at each other. Ready to work, Valerie asked "Where do we start?" Mr. Dulany said, "We did the hard work last week, turning the dirt over in the buckets and removing any old leaves and debris left over from the long frigid winter."

Uninterrupted, Mr. Dulany continued while his small gardening protégé listened intently. "If you noticed on the picnic table, I have all the plants that are mature enough to be planted outside. There are tomatoes, peppers and cucumbers today. All with have to do is dig a small hole in the dirt, gently grab one plant, spread the roots, put a handful of Miracle Gro plant food in the hole, put the plant in the hole, cover the roots, pack the dirt around the base of the plants and give it a nice cool cup of water."

Valerie looked at the picnic table, Valerie looked at Mr. Dulany. "There are so many plants, this will take all day!" she proclaimed. "You can stop anytime, but honestly, this won't take long. Together if we work hard and stay focused, it will take about an hour, hopefully your parents are home then." Deciding to count the plants Valerie was astonished how all the plants were green, but the leaves were all different. Separating the plants Valerie announced "35 tomato plants, 12 cucumber plants, 4 onion plants, 12 green bell peppers, 10 banana peppers and 6 jalapeno pepper plants and four small envelopes. Thinking quickly, she added the plants together. "That's 79 plants, we better get to work."

Taking the small shovel and a tomato plant, Valerie headed to the garden. Curiosity finally caught up with her, boldly she questioned Mr. Dulany about the envelopes. "What's in the envelopes?" she asked. Being honest and candid, Mr. Dulany answered her, "The grey envelope has sunflower seeds, the brown one has green beans and the green one has pumpkin seeds."

Being a stickler for details, Valerie corrected Mr. Dulany, "but there are four envelopes." Thinking, Mr. Dulany was baffled. "Okay, you're right! The blue envelope has a sunflower seed, the green one has a green beans seed, the grey has a pumpkin seed, and the brown envelope has a "magic" seed in it"

Laughing, Valerie repeated "Magic." Embarrassed, Mr. Dulany said "the cashier at Amanda's Nursery wanted a donation for the animal homeless shelter on North Avenue. Valerie was impressed. Her name was

Kaylee, and she would not let me check out until I gave a "donation". I decided just to give her five dollars for the "donation." In appreciation, of my "donation" she gave me the green envelope and said there was a magic seed in the envelope, but be very, very careful. I laughed'

Confused, Valerie corrected Mr. Dulany again. "I thought you said the green envelope had the pumpkin seeds, the brown one had the sunflower seeds, and the green envelope had the green beans." "If I remember right, I said the blue envelope has the sunflower seeds, the green one has the pumpkin seeds, and the brown envelope contained the green beans" insisted Mr. Dulany. Being persistent in her quest for knowledge, Valerie asked "So, what's in the grey envelope?"

Valerie did well in school. She excelled in math, English, social studies, she was an honor student. Realizing daylight was slowly disappearing, Mr. Dulany decided he needed to get back to planting. "We save the seeds for last, all we need to do is poke a small hole in the dirt, put the seed in and cover the seed with dirt. Keep the soil moist and they grow very quickly, very, very quickly."

Together, under the warm Saturday sun, they worked in Mr. Dulany's garden. First, they planted the 35 tomato plants. As instructed by Mr. Dulany, Valerie gave each one a drink of water and put a tomato cage on each plant. Next was the 12 cucumber plants, then the 28 assorted pepper plants. Being extremely delicate and small, Mr. Dulany let Valerie transfer the tiny onion plants.

Mr. Dulany was right, it took, 53 minutes to plant the 79 plants. Valerie was an excellent worker. In anticipation of her parents coming home she wanted to finish the job. Valerie never left any job without finishing, not homework, not chores, her motto was "no job left behind." However, Mr. Dulany was hot and extremely exhausted. "Thank goodness, we are done for the day" proudly proclaimed Mr. Dulany. "Let's celebrate with some ice-cold Lipton Peach Iced Tea!" He headed for his back-kitchen door.

Realizing that Mr. Dulany had not planted the seeds from the envelopes. Worried that they were not going to finish the job, Valerie pleaded with Mr. Dulany. "WE STILL NEED TO PLANT THE PUMPKINS, SUNFLOWERS and BEANS!"

Mr. Dulany was tired. He had been working all morning long, mowing, trimming and pulling weeds. "We can finish tomorrow, let us take a break. Please. sit down, relax and I will be back with peach tea and some chips, what do you like Fritos? Takis? Pringles?" Not waiting for an answer Mr. Dulany walked inside his back door to his kitchen.

Disappointed, Valerie looked at the four envelopes. "He said poke a hole in the dirt, put the seed in, cover the seed and water. Trying to impress Mr. Dulany, Valerie knew she had little time. Grabbing the four envelopes Valerie tried to remember what was in each envelope. She opened-up the green envelope there was one seed, in the blue envelope there was one seed, the brown envelope had one seed and the grey envelope had one seed, what was a girl supposed to do?

Suddenly, Mr. Dulany appeared out his back door, "It seems we are out of peach iced tea how will Orange Crush do?" Nervously, Valerie quickly hid the open envelopes behind her back and bashfully answered "Sure, Orange Crush is fine, take your time!"

As Mr. Dulany closed the kitchen door, Valerie foresaw the future, it was disastrous. She had turned the envelopes upside down, dropping the seeds on the patio. Scurrying to pick up the seeds and put them back into the correct envelopes Valerie forgot the chosen colors. Did the pumpkin seed go in the green envelope or the blue? Did the sunflower seed go in the blue envelope or the grey? How about the green bean seed, did the seed go in the brown or blue envelope? It did not matter; she did not know the difference between the four seeds she picked up. Which one was the sunflower? Which one was the green bean? Which one was the pumpkin? The clock was ticking. If Mr. Dulany came out, he would be disappointed that she did not listen. Springing into action, she grabbed the four seeds and started to plant the seeds, poke a hole, put the seed in, cover it, water it, done. Seed number 2, poke a hole in the dirt, put the seed in, cover it and water it, done. Seed 3, poke a hole in the dirt, put the seed in the hole, cover it and then it hit her, there were four seeds. What happened to the fourth seed? Did she drop it? Ignoring the aspect of a fourth seed, she watered the third seed. Taking a deep breath, she took a big step back admiring her work, proud of her work. Then bucket number 3 started to shake.

Bucket number 3 with seed number 3 shook, it rattled and burped. Finally, quieting down, Valerie was relieved. Then like a rocket ship blasting into space, the plant started to grow. Quickly, the bean stalk grew to a foot tall, then it doubled to two feet tall, then four, then eight, then sixteen, thirty-two, sixty-four, one hundred twenty-eight feet tall. It seemed to keep doubling as it reached higher and higher into the bright blue sky.

Valerie was shocked. Valerie was scared. She tried calling Mr. Dulany, but no words came out. Valerie just stared at the beanstalk. It was huge, it was humongous, it was awesome. Talking to herself she wondered if all the plants grew like this, what was in the soil? Would Mr. Dulany be mad? Walking closer to the oversized plant Valerie heard someone saying "Climb me, climb me! The world awaits you! Hypnotized by the voice, Valerie started to climb the beanstalk. Higher and higher she climbed.

Mr. Dulany came out of his house. Carrying the tray of Orange Crush glasses with a bowl each of Fritos, Takis and Pringles he went to the patio table calling, "Valerie, snacks are ready!"

Garbanzo Beans

Valerie was excited. As she climbed the giant beanstalk, she wondered how much further she would go. As she looked down, she saw the tiny grey and white barn that was in Mr. Dulany's yard. "Mr. Dulany, I didn't tell him I was going up a beanstalk, he is going to be frantic." Reaching for her cell phone stuffed in her back-pocket, Valerie stopped and began to dial his number 555- 390-1630 Then her right foot slipped on a small wet leaf, desperately trying to hold on, instinctively with both of her tiny hands, she firmly grabbed the center stalk. Fortunately, she saved herself from plunging back down to earth, unfortunately she did not hold on to her cell phone with the Kate Spade case which contained her Hallsberry School identification. She watched as the cell phone went plunging down to earth, falling to certain destruction.

"Valerie, Valerie!" called Mr. Dulany "Snacks are ready, I have some nice cold Orange Crush and some snacks." Still there was no Valerie. "Valerie did you go back to your house? He questioned loudly. Mr. Dulany remained surprisingly calm although he was praying for Vivian's safety. As Mr. Dulany tried to remain calm, he looked around his backyard for any clues to Valerie's sudden disappearance. He turned and saw the Little Tikes log cabin, but she would never hide in there. Too many spiders.

VALERIE AND THE BEANSTALK

Suspicious of a crime, Mr. Dulany wanted to leave no stone unturned. He stared at the picnic table, and he noticed the envelopes were opened with the seeds missing. Continuing to turn clockwise, he noticed the obvious, it was almost a crime, the second to last cherry tomato plant did not have a tomato cage. Trying to do the right thing, he immediately retrieved a tomato cage from behind the shed. "Valerie!" he called still looking for his neighbor. Proud of his garden, proud of Valerie, Mr. Dulany admired the work they had accomplished. Then it was like a miracle falling from the sky, something suddenly hit the ground making a loud thud, scaring Mr. Dulany.

Rushing over to the object, he picked up the broken cell phone and holder. Shattered beyond recognition, the cell phone was useless, however, the Kate Spade holder contained an identification and a credit card both with Valerie's name on them. He looked up and noticed the large beanstalk. Mr. Dulany was amazed how tall the beanstalk was. He wondered if Valerie tried climbing it.

"Keep climbing Valerie, Keep climbing", the female voice said to Valerie. Valerie was getting tired, she looked down again and saw only a faint glimpse of her family's roof top. Fascinated at the view, she looked for Camilla's house and Aaliyah's rooftop. Determined, to make it to the top, Valerie continued her journey to the top of the beanstalk. However, her body was not cooperating, her arms were getting weak, her legs were burning with pain and with the lack of warm air in the lower atmosphere, she was getting cold. Giving her the encouragement, she desperately needed to continue, the female voice sweetly announced, "You are so close, just a little further, keep coming to a place where Valerie is a Queen, keep climbing." All she needed to hear was Queen Valerie, those two words gave her the burst of energy she needed to prolong this unbelievable journey.

Mr. Dulany looked up at the giant beanstalk. In his heart, he knew Valerie climbed the giant beanstalk. Should he call 911? Would 911 believe him? Would 911 laugh at him when he mentioned Valerie climbing a "giant" beanstalk? Mr. Dulany knew the answers. He had to go find Valerie, without any help before she got hurt, he had to go find Valerie before her parents came home, he had to find Valerie, now. Without regard for his own safety, Mr. Dulany began the most dangerous excursion of his life, he began to climb the giant beanstalk.

Almost out of breath, almost out of energy, Valerie finally reached the cloud. "Congratulations, you made it!" exclaimed an eerily familiar voice. Cautiously stepping off the beanstalk, Valerie gently stepped on the cloud, making sure it was secure. Prudently, she took every step seriously. Through the foggy mist of the clouds Valerie marched gallantly forward on her unbelievable journey. Then almost magically appearing out the foggy mist, Valerie saw it. It was beautiful, it was massive, it had her name on the entrance door. Queen Valerie's Castle.

Mr. Dulany was no spring chicken, but what he lacked in youth, he made up in energy and endurance. He was tall, 6'3" and was often called the midnight ghost, because of the time he started work and the incredible pace he created for himself. Younger men were amazed, older men were jealous, but he did not mind the teasing, this was the way God made him and he was proud of his athletic abilities. He analyzed the humongous beanstalk, he hoisted himself up to the first branch. Never looking back, he began his rescue mission to save Valerie.

Great Northern

Queen Valerie's Castle, it had a certain ring to it. Valerie thought about being a Queen, she had worked hard all her life, she deserved what she was going to get. She was an outstanding student, a fabulous friend, a devoted daughter and a superior sister. The ten-year-old thought she knew everything; she was a natural born leader. As she walked closer to the castle, random people cheered. The two big brown castle doors were opened by two very serious royal guards, Brandon and Caiden.

Overwhelmed with happiness, Valerie could not believe what she was happening. Sophia and Abigail were holding a large banner saying "Congratulations". Sammy and David were holding a dozen helium balloons, two royal purple, two light blue, two rose red, two emerald green and two sunshine yellow, topped off with and shiny silver balloon with "You're #1" Valerie was impressed. Her wishes were becoming true. Suddenly a young woman came running up to her.

Mr. Dulany was making great progress in his travels. Having a sense of urgency to save his neighbor and friend, Mr. Dulany hustled up the beanstalk. Step by step, branch by branch, Mr. Dulany worked his way up the giant beanstalk, hoping to catch and rescue Valerie. However, age was catching up to him, his mind was younger than his body. It was a long way up and he was getting slower and slower, but he would never quit, never.

The woman rushed over to Valerie. The guards did not try to stop her, she carried a paper filled clipboard, a blue Paper mate pen and a smile that would melt a steel block. This was not a friendly smile it was a mean devious scowl, and it came at her swiftly. Introducing herself as only Thalia, she told Valerie she was in-charge of this magical beanstalk and everything she had experienced so far would stop until the papers were signed, for legal purposes, of course.

Confused about signing "Papers" Valerie was stunned. "It's a safety measure for the lawyers, dot a few I's, cross a few t's and sign a few papers and we resume the festivities. I am your friend, probably your new best friend, look what I have given you, everything you have wished for." Valerie's kryptonite was reading. She did not like to read and did not do it unless somebody made her. Valerie trusted her new best friend. Valerie signed every piece of paper without reading any of it, nobody made her. Handing Thalia back her clipboard and pen, Queen Valerie announced, "let the party begin!"

Mr. Dulany was making progress. In his heart, he realized he had done this to Valerie. "Why did I use that new Miracle Gro special plant food? Who knew that it would work so well? Why did I leave her alone outside? It's all my fault!" Mr. Dulany started to tear up, so much he could not see. It did not matter, all he had to was rescue Valerie, all he had to was go was up. Step by step, branch by branch he took, determined to find Valerie.

The party for Queen Valerie continued. Everyone wanted to greet the new Queen, people loved Valerie. Who would not? She was young, pretty and incredibly friendly. However, she was getting hungry, it was well past lunchtime. Trying to find her "new" best friend, Thalia, was impossible. The crowd was thick with adoring fans. Queen Valerie thought about Thalia, there was something about her, it is almost like she knew her, but Valerie could not place a finger on it.

The castle doors suddenly closed. Queen Valerie wondered what was going on. The sky started to rumble, the wind began to roar and appearing out of nowhere a helicopter appeared. Trying to land the mighty helicopter was nearly impossible, but the royal guards, Paris and Sophia, eventually cleared a spot for the flying machine. From a distance Queen Valerie squinted her big brown eyes and saw it was a Grub Hub delivery.

Wishing it were for her, Queen Valerie's stomach roared viciously. The Royal Guard to Queen Valerie's left, Crystal, was astonished with the huge noise coming from the tiny Queen, she tried not to laugh, but failed. Queen Valerie continued to squint at the helicopter, finally noticing her new best friend Thalia, rushing to the open door of the helicopter where she grabbed a Panda Express bag from the helicopter pilot, Samantha.

Exhausted beyond words, Mr. Dulany finally reached the cloud. He did not know if Valerie was here or not, but he had to check. Fatigued, Mr. Dulany, took both his arms and grabbed the edge of the cloud, struggling, he hoisted his left leg to the edge of the fluffy cloud. Unsuccessful, he used his arms and pulled with everything he had to pull himself up. Trying again, he lifted his tired left leg and painfully dragged the limb above the edge of the cloud. All that was left was his right leg, which came up with more effort and labor then Mr. Dulany had in him. Finally, off the beanstalk and onto the soft fluffy cloud, Mr. Dulany collapsed in a heap of tired body parts.

After Thalia grabbed the Panda Express bag from the helicopter pilot, she stood back and allowed Samantha to takeoff. Men held their hats, women controlled their hair and the children, Melina, Layla and Leah, covered their eyes as the rotor controlling the blades started to spin. Faster and faster the blades turned causing a small windstorm, finally the helicopter flew straight up and away.

With the helicopter gone, Thalia quickly took the Panda Express bag and ran over to Queen Valerie. Snapping her fingers as a command, Thalia waited by Valerie, not saying a word. Within seconds, two of the royal guards, Elena and Ailin came racing with a table and a chair. Closely behind came a waitress, Amiya, Queen Valerie was amazed at how much the waitress looked like her mom. The waitress quickly put an aqua blue linen tablecloth on the table, followed by a light blue placement. Like a fine oiled machine, Amiya swiftly laid down the gold trimmed china plate, complimented with the finest silverware, a fork, spoon and knife. Finishing off the presentation another waiter, Giselle, came by with cold glasses and filled them with ice cold peach iced tea, Queen Valerie's favorite.

Queen Valerie was impressed with the unbelievable service and the unbelievable attention to detail. Queen Valerie wished this happened at home. Suddenly, Thalia ordered Queen Valerie to sit down and enjoy her lunch. "But I didn't order lunch!" Queen Valerie exclaimed. Thalia said she did, earlier. Then the waitress plated the bag from Panda Express, it was an order of orange chicken with half fried rice and half chow Mein noodles, Valerie's absolute favorite.

Thinking to herself, Queen Valerie wondered how Thalia knew. But really, Queen Valerie did not care, she was savoring the incredible meal from Panda Express. It was not the Veggie pizza that Vivian liked, and received, it was what Queen Valerie wished for, and received.

Still exhausted Mr. Dulany did not move. Still exhausted Mr. Dulany slept. Still exhausted Mr. Dulany would not be rescuing Valerie anytime soon.

Kidney Beans

Full of her Orange chicken lunch, Queen Valerie, pushed her chair away from the table. Thanking them for lunch and their hospitality, Queen Valerie said she needed to go back home. She thought of Mr. Dulany who was probably still looking for her, she should not have gone up the beanstalk without telling him. She thought of Mom, Dad and Vivian, they might be looking for after their trip to Target.

Thinking quick, Thalia snapped her fingers. Pulling up was a brand new green 2020 Subaru Sedan, complete with a manual transmission. Thalia began to speak, just as you wished, but since you are too young to drive the car comes with a handsome young chauffer named Colhane, he will take you anywhere. The handsome Colhane came out from the driver's seat. Valerie smiled and her knees went weak. Opening the passenger's seat, Colhane gestured for Valerie to get in, it was useless to fight the powers of Colhane, so she sat down.

Colhane gently closed the door. He himself got in, buckled up and revved the engine, showing off the power of the car. He shifted to drive and asked, "Where to Queen?" Memorized by his big brown eyes, Queen Valerie was rendered speechless. Having been instructed by Thalia, Colhane knew exactly where to take Queen Valerie, "I know" suggested Colhane, "How about a trip to the nail salon?" Melting, like a stick of butter on the hot sidewalk in the middle of July, Valerie looked at her hands and sweetly said "You know me so well." Nervously, she twirled her messy hair. "Your wish is my command" Colhane answered and drove, speeding all the way to the nail salon.

Driving inappropriately fast but making all the green lights Valerie was amazed at Colhane's driving ability. "You are a very lucky driver, we made it in record time" complimented Queen Valerie. A bit bashful, Colhane quickly replied, "it's got nothing to do with luck, it's Thalia's magic." Colhane quickly parked the Subaru, got out and gallantly opened the door for Queen Valerie. Elegantly, Queen Valerie stood up and was escorted down a luxurious red carpet, into the nail salon where she was greeted by Esmeralda, the salon's owner.

"Welcome to Esmeralda's Nail Salon, where beauty has no price," said a very relaxed Esmeralda. Her assistant Ayesha quickly brought Queen Valerie over to the VIP area, sat her down and got her a cold peach iced tea. Like an explosion, the front door quickly opened bringing Thalia and another person. "What brings you here?" Thalia quickly answered, "This is JJ, he is one of my most trusted assistants, and do I need a reason to see my new best friend?"

Being totally professional, Ayesha and Esmeralda, started the manicure and pedicure. Taking Valerie's glass of peach tea and setting it on the table, Ayesha leaned the chair back and put a large white cotton towel over Queen Valerie's clothes. Esmeralda grabbed Queen Valerie's right hand and immediately sighed, "What have you been doing? Digging in Dirt?" Queen Valerie was not paying attention, she was focused on Thalia and JJ.

Not waiting for an answer, Esmeralda told Ayesha this Queen needed the Super Deluxe Package. Ayesha was now working on the pedicure for her feet, quickly agreed. Queen Valerie was too focused on trying to hear Thalia, Valerie turned her head a little to hear better. Thalia saw Valerie eavesdropping on her conversation, so she took JJ outside for a very private conversation.

Meanwhile, Esmeralda and Ayesha went to work. Ayesha on the pedicure, Esmeralda on the manicure. "This is going to take a while would you like a facial too?" Ayesha asked. "Certainly!" answered The Queen. Esmeralda quickly got the cucumbers from the refrigerator and the special homemade facial cleaner. It was made of mayonnaise, guacamole, and Italian salad dressing. The cucumbers moisturized the eyes, while the facial cleaner exfoliated, scrubbed and moisturized the face.

Both girls knew Queen Valerie never had a professional manicure and pedicure. After years of neglect and self-manicuring it was their job to clean up the mess and make Queen Valerie glamourous. Phase 1, demolition, they had to clean the nails with nail polish remover, then clip, file and buff the nails, care for the cuticles, exfoliate the hands and feet then they needed to moisturize the skin and cuticles. If all went well, they would begin Phase 2, construction. No permits were needed, just a lot of prayer. Phase 2 involved applying a base coat, applying the first coat of color, applying a second coat, applying a top clear protective coat and finally, cleaning up the mess and letting the nails dry.

Outside, JJ and Thalia talked. "This is going so well, Valerie signed the papers, giving away her freedom. Kids who do not read are easy targets. Soon because of her bad attitude, she will become one of our slaves forever. A few more wishes granted, and she will begin spending her days searching for helium for me. I do not know why, but she irritates me, I think I will start her at the bottom of the cave, where it is especially dark and dirty. Without helium our cloud will cease to exist. JJ, I need you to make sure the shopping spree goes perfect and her fantasy excursion to the Philippines is the perfect trip."

JJ was confused, "Once she gets off the plane from the Philippines, she loses her family and her freedom? That seems a little extreme. She has been cooped up in her house for two months because of the pandemic, she's only ten, she made a mistake." Thalia was getting angry, "Are you disobeying me? Questioning my authority? All actions have consequences!" Frightened, JJ answered "No, I will obey you Almighty Queen Thalia ruler of the Cloud of Thalia". Then in a sign of respect JJ bowed down to the powerful Queen Thalia.

Finally rested, Mr. Dulany began to awake. "What have I done? I have slept, I have done nothing to rescue Valerie. She's probably alone, hungry and scared, I need to find and help her!" Feeling refreshed, he got himself up and started walking on the cloud, hoping to find some trace of Valerie.

Black-Eyed Beans

Queen Valerie was enjoying her wonderful day at the nail salon. It was all about Valerie, nothing more needed to be said. Almost done, Esmeralda showed Queen Valerie a bottle of OPI white nail polish and gracefully asked "Do you still want to go with this color or do want to go with something a little flashier, like a hot pink or maybe gothic black or the most popular choice, the rainbow?" Queen Valerie immediately answered, "Oh no, my wish has always been to have a professional manicure and pedicure with OPI white nail polish. It goes with everything, somebody once said it's a classic."

Esmeralda and Ayesha applied the two coats of the OPI white nail polish. Queen Valerie was right, it looked fabulous. Esmeralda finished by covering the nail polish with the clearcoat. Meanwhile Ayesha took the cucumbers off Queen Valerie's eyes and began to remove the "homemade" facial cleaner. Getting a mirror so Queen Valerie could see herself, Esmeralda was proud of their work, Ayesha finished cleaning the room.

Next came the hair stylist, in walked Bella, short for Isabella. Straight from Glendale Heights, she looked, she gazed, she poked, she prodded. Bella suddenly snapped her fingers, in walked Jaz, her assistant. Bella whispered in Jaz's ear. Before Bella and Jaz started their magic, Queen Valerie suddenly announced, "I want to go home!" Jaz immediately replied,

PART TWO

"Bella has a reputation she says you are not going anywhere until your hair is shampooed, conditioned, dried and brushed."

Esmeralda joined the conversation. "As the future Queen of this great Land, you must look fabulous at all times." Valerie heard the word, future, and questioned Esmeralda, "Future?" Appearing out of nowhere, JJ, appeared and said, "your official coronation is not until you get back from the Philippines, then your life will change forever" Then JJ took Esmeralda to the back room, where she was quickly dismissed from her duties as a beautician and sent to the helium mines.

Jaz looked at Queen Valerie's hair, Bella looked at Queen Valerie's hair. Jaz walked around Queen Valerie, touching, feeling and smelling the Queen's hair. Bella walked around Queen Valerie, touching, feeling and smelling the Queen's hair. "I know," said a confident Jaz. "I know," said a confident Bella.

Jaz declared "I shall make her hair a bright fluorescent pink, perfect for this Queen." "A bold choice" replied Bella. Bella then declared "I shall make her hair an electric purple, perfect for this Queen" "A bold choice" replied Jaz. "Curly" answered Jaz. "Curly" agreed Bella. "Mohawk" answered Jaz. "Mohawk" agreed Bella. "Tattoo" answered Jaz.

Over-hearing their conversation, JJ urgently walked back in the room. This is Queen Valerie, there will be no pink nor purple hair, there will be no curls, no mohawk and no tattoo. Valerie is a queen not a punk rocker, she must always look and act of authority. Keep her hair straight, do not cut it. Make it a dark chocolate brown, no better yet make it an ashy brown. That's an order!"

Finally, Jaz and Bella were done, Ayesha was done. watching their words very carefully, Bella asked Queen Valerie to shut her eyes and handed her the royal golden mirror. Bella continued "You have been beautified, elengantied, prettified, and glamourized, what do you think?" Valerie opened her pretty big brown eyes and stared at the magical mirror.

"OMG!" exclaimed an enthusiastic Queen Valerie, "I look fabulous, I have been Fabulized!" "Now Can I go home?"

JJ and Thalia suddenly came coming running into the salon. "Why do you want to go home?" asked a very concerned Thalia. Trying to save his job, JJ interrupted Thalia, "Queen Valerie, this is your home now, where your wishes have come true." Pulling out all the stops JJ continued "Aren't you happy here? Every time Thalia senses that you are not happy, she will be here. She's like your mom, she has a six sense of when somethings wrong."

Letting JJ do his job, Thalia remained quiet. Twisting his words JJ continued "I promise you after your one-hour unlimited online Target shopping spree, and your trip to the Philippines, you will be done." "You had me at unlimited Target online shopping spree!" exclaimed the recently fabulized Queen Valerie. Knowing JJ had everything under control, Thalia left. Suddenly, the ground shook and knocked everyone down.

Thalia began to panic. Only she knew what this meant, her cloud was running out of helium. Thalia had to leave to put pressure on the helium diggers, those despondent greedy children who never appreciated what their parents did for them. Those ungrateful children who wished for a better life, were known on the Cloud of Thalia as "The Wishers."

The Wishers had to find more helium. The Wishers had to dig deeper. The Wishers had to work harder and faster. Desperate, Thalia knew if the Wishers did not find helium soon her cloud would begin to sink.

Mr. Dulany who was walking down the path to the castle was also knocked down with the force of the cloud shaking. Relentless in his pursuit of finding Valerie, he got himself up off the soft cushy ground and continued. Although he was not wearing his glasses, he saw a large building ahead, not sure of what it was he had stumbled upon, a fort, a mansion or maybe he thought it was a mirage.

Hope, a small clue, that is all he needed. Valerie was a unique neighbor, Valerie and Mr. Dulany had a special relationship. She would always help him, with whatever he needed, the garbage, his writing, the garden, this made him smile. She gave him a huge hug whenever they saw each other. Once Valerie wrote him a note, saying he was her favorite and what a difference he has made in her life. Mr. Dulany still has that note using it as an example to himself of how he can be with all children. Finding Valerie was his only goal. He needed to stay relentless in his pursuit of Valerie.

Finally reaching the building, Mr. Dulany was relieved, maybe they knew where Valerie was. The shaking of the cloud knocked down Valerie's sign, Mr. Dulany did not know where he was, he knocked on the large door. Nobody answered, impatiently he knocked again. The giant door began to open by two very large guards, Deisy and Jaselyn. Mr. Dulany was tall, but they were taller. Mr. Dulany was big, but they were bigger. Many children thought Mr. Dulany was scary, but they were scarier. Without saying a word, the two guards let Mr. Dulany in and quickly closed the castle doors. Mr. Dulany was not scared.

Dirty, sweaty, and completely disheveled, Mr. Dulany hesitantly walked in and looked around. He saw an empty courtyard; little did he know Thalia ordered all the townspeople to work the mines to find helium. Suddenly, a young woman walked over to Mr. Dulany. "Hello, my name is Thalia. How can I help you?"

Quite surprised at the greeting from Thalia, Mr. Dulany relaxed and thought he could trust Thalia, she was very pretty, very nice, and a had great smile, a combination that was Mr. Dulany's kryptonite. Mr. Dulany started to ramble, "there was gardening, the seeds, the beanstalk, young girl, lost, scared, hungry." Realizing the stranger was talking about Valerie, Thalia immediately offered him some food and water. "Come with me, I will help you!"

Tired, Mr. Dulany followed his new friend Thalia, hoping to find Valerie, rescue Valerie and take Valerie back home, where she belonged. Thalia had other plans for Mr. Dulany. Being very pleasant, Thalia escorted Mr. Dulany to a small dingy room with no windows. Politely, she asked him to go in, sensing danger, Mr. Dulany said he preferred not to. As Mr. Dulany investigated the dark room, he was ambushed by one of the royal guards, Deisy who violently pushed him into the room. Then the unthinkable, the door was slammed shut and locked with a massive thick lock.

Thalia had the key. She ordered the taller guard Jaselyn to immediately take the key and give it to JJ, "Tell him to get rid of this prisoner by the end of the day, he is too old and weak to work the mines!" Like a desperate Queen on a mission, Thalia left for the helium mines.

12

Fava Beans

Jaselyn entered the salon quietly and mysteriously. JJ did not understand why the royal guard had left her post, so he immediately excused himself to find out what was going on. Suddenly the ground shook again and again. Jaselyn stood strong; JJ kept his footing. The tremors stopped. JJ went to Jaselyn and asked her why she was there.

Quietly Jaselyn whispered into JJ ear, "Queen Thalia went to the helium mines, she will not be back until late, Queen Thalia has a prisoner, an unwanted guest, and the Queen has ordered you to get rid of him tonight." Here is the key to his cell. Jaselyn handed the key to JJ and immediately returned to her post. Upset, JJ began talking under his breath "When is it my job to get rid of prisoners? When do I need a key? I have a key to every door, lock and gate on this cloud!" Insulted, he slammed the big brass key onto the salon counter, where he inadvertently left it.

Hearing everything Jaselyn and JJ were saying, Queen Valerie was enlightened, she had to get that key. The "unwanted" guest had to be Mr. Dulany. Excited he came to get her Queen Valerie knew something was wrong. Trusting no one at this point, coming up with a plan to get the key was easy, Queen Valerie asked JJ, "Whatever happened to the dessert I wished for lunch?" JJ knew nothing. Trying to appease the Queen Valerie, JJ asked "What did you wish for dessert?"

Being a bit dramatic, Queen Valerie rubbed her chin, then scratched her head, pondered and began speaking. "I think it was peppermint ice cream, no, maybe it was a large slice of turtle cheesecake topped with red ripened sliced strawberries. Before leaving JJ asked, "will that be all?" Queen Valerie shook her head yes. JJ began to leave again. Queen Valerie commanded "STOP" JJ stopped immediately. Queen Valerie politely said, "I think I was wrong, my choice was a large piece of chocolate chocolate chip Bundt cake, actually get a slice of chocolate chocolate chip Bundt cake for everyone." JJ quickly left. With the girls in the backroom of the nail salon, Queen Valerie quietly stood up and meandered over to counter and quickly snatched the large brass key.

With perfect timing, Queen Valerie sat down, JJ came back to the salon with two pastry chefs, Emma and Soha. Meanwhile, Ayesha, Jaz and Bella returned from the nail salon's back room. Queen Valerie declared "Chocolate chocolate chip Bundt cake is twice as good when shared with friends. Everybody, please have a slice." Naimah followed with cold glasses of milk. JJ wondered why Queen Thalia would send somebody this nice to the helium mines.

Under strict orders by Queen Thalia, JJ tried keeping Queen Valerie on schedule, next was her one-hour unlimited Target online shopping spree. Feeling the big key in her pocket, Queen Valerie was nervous, she wondered what door the key went to, she wondered who the unwanted guest was, she needed to search the cloud. Suddenly the cloud shook for a few seconds and Queen Valerie felt like the cloud dropped a few inches, again.

JJ politely insisted that the Queen Valerie finish her dessert. It was time for the one-hour Target unlimited shopping spree. The only computer that was hooked up to the internet was in Queen Thalia's office, all the way across the cloud. Nobody else needed the internet, most visitors here were here because they did not appreciate what they had, they were greedy and wanted more, without working for it. They were the "The Wishers". They were prisoners, all they did was dig for helium for Queen Thalia, all day, every day. Ailin came to pick up the dishes.

Queen Valerie was excited. The recently glamourized and fabulized young lady was ready to make her first public appearance. "Can I get a tour of my castle on the way to the computer?" asked a very curious Queen Valerie! Trying to stay focused, JJ insisted they keep on schedule or Thalia would be mad. Trying to be funny, Queen Valerie replied, "What she going to do throw you in the dungeon?"

JJ's reaction was startling. He knew the dungeon, where Mr. Dulany stayed was just a one-day visit, after that you were removed. Worse was the lifetime sentence of working the helium mines. Cold, dark and dirty, 18 hours a day, digging for helium. JJ wondered why he did not appreciate what his parents gave him, now he was one of "The Wishers", a glorified wisher who worked for Queen Thalia. He knew if he did not do exactly as Queen Thalia ordered, he would be back in the helium minds too.

The Royal Guard Amaris helped Queen Valerie up. JJ politely encouraged Queen Valerie to get her list so they could walk over to Thalia's office and use the computer. JJ promised he would give her the tour as they walked. Queen Valerie was so excited she "accidently" left her shopping list by the salon chair. Queen Valerie loved Target and whenever she thought of something that she needed she put on the list that she carried everywhere. She said "Thank you and goodbye" to Ayesha, Jaz and Bella.

Amaris and JJ led the small group on the tour of the cloud, followed by Queen Valerie and another very quiet guard Clemente. JJ walked and talked. There was not much here, a big bedroom filled with maybe a couple hundred beds, a kitchen where Citlali and Corey were preparing lunch for someone. Nothing unusual, no dungeon, no Mr. Dulany.

Mad at himself, Mr. Dulany sat in the corner of his cell and cried. He came to rescue Valerie. Now he was being held prisoner in a dark, cold dungeon. He worried about his poor innocent helpless friend. Valerie was out there, hungry, cold and without a friend. Mr. Dulany had a deep voice, a voice so deep it did not carry, yelling would be of no use, but he had to try. Wiping the tears from his red eyes, Mr. Dulany went by the small window by the front door and started screaming "Valerie! Valerie! Valerie! Ashley, the guard, ordered Mr. Dulany to stop. Mr. Dulany took a deep breath and started screaming at the top of his lungs "Valerie! Valerie! Valerie!"

Being deep in the center of the castle tour, Valerie realized this was the perfect time to tell JJ she "accidently" forgot her list at the nail salon. Turning her acting abilities on full throttle, Valerie started to check her pockets, they were empty. Seeing Queen Valerie in despair, JJ came to her aid, JJ asked "Is there a problem?" Bashfully, with a twinkle in her big brown eyes she told JJ she "accidently" forgot the shopping list at the nail salon. Like a knight in shining armor, JJ left to retrieve the list.

With only the two guards watching her, Queen Valerie turned on the charm. Clemente stood strong and said nothing. Amaris was easily distracted talking about the weather, Thalia and being a Wisher. Valerie was too busy looking for Mr. Dulany to hear anything she had to say. Finally, quiet, Valerie could now hear a pin drop. Then she thought her name was being called, she finally focused on the voice coming at her, then the voice stopped.

As he continued to scream a group of royal guards quickly opened the dungeon door. Shayaan, Declan and Tykie all rushed Mr. Dulany. Mr. Dulany fell backwards hitting his head against the concrete wall, knocking him unconscious. "That will shut him up for a few hours!" proudly exclaimed one of the guards.

Meanwhile, Queen Thalia was on the other side of the cloud. "The Wishers" were knee deep in dirt, they were hungry, they were thirsty, they were tired, but Queen Thalia did not care. With a bullhorn in one hand and a whip in the other she demanded that they work harder and faster. She yelled into the bullhorn, "Let's go Wishers, find that helium" she cracked he whip trying to intimidate them. Then the cloud shook again. Queen Thalia yelled more, demanding more.

Worried about Queen Valerie, JJ came running. He knew the real queen, Queen Thalia, would be back soon and he needed to have the shopping spree finished, Queen Thalia needed another strong young person to work the helium mines. The helium was running out, time was running out.

JJ handed Queen Valerie's long shopping list. JJ was surprised a ten-year-old Queen could want so much from a store like Target. The arm's length list was surprisingly filled with everything from food to tools, she was greedy too, he began to understand why Queen Thalia chose her to become the next "Wisher".

Adzuki Beans

Before going in the Thalia's extravagant office, JJ warned Queen Valerie. "Stay focused, don't be distracted. Do not worry about what Thalia has or does not have. Once I say go, you will have exactly one hour to finish shopping. At the end of one hour, you will have exactly 15 minutes to pack and board a plane for the Philippines, your final wish. Anything left in carts before the time runs out you will not receive. All the credit card information is preprogrammed." JJ quickly turned on the Apple computer and immediately went to Target.com and logged in for Queen Valerie. "Please sit down on the count of three, 1,2, 3, GO!" instructed JJ.

Valerie was an unusually organized for a ten-year-old. Her shoes in her closet were organized by color and style. Her desk at Hallsberry School was organized very neatly, not only by subject but also by the time of day, she was Mrs. Marino's model student. This Target shopping spree would be no different, organization was the key. Queen Valerie had four sections she would be shopping for, 15 minutes each category. JJ put his feet up on the desk and had Dayamin get him an ice-cold Pepsi.

First up on the list, Queen Valerie was shopping for the families of Hallsberry School. She had to focus on non-perishable food items, healthy non-perishable food items. 10 cases each of Green Giant corn, beans and carrots, in the cart. Next up was 10 cases each Cheerios, Wheaties and

Corn Flakes. Next, she had 10 cases peanut butter granola bars, followed by 10 cases Planter's peanuts. Having less than five minutes left she went to the pasta section where she ordered 15 cases angel hair pasta, 15 cases spaghetti, 15 cases Kraft macaroni and cheese and 30 cases Ragu pasta sauce. Time was out. She clicked the "place order now" button.

Within seconds, the USPS, United States Postal Service helicopter pilot was outside Thalia's office ringing the doorbell. JJ was startled and ran to the door. "Hello, I am Sammy and I have a delivery for Hallsberry School and Queen Valerie." While Queen Valerie worked on the next project, her dad, JJ told Sammy to put the box in the corner of the office. Sammy did as he was told and filled half the office. JJ was amazed and told himself "Maybe, just maybe, I misjudged Queen Valerie".

Next up on the list was her dad. First, she went to the automotive department and ordered him some seat covers, steering wheel covers and floormats for his stick shift Subaru sedan. It had been a while since Dad washed his car, so she placed some car wash and wax, complete with brushes into the cart. It had been years since Dad had treated himself to any new clothes, so she ordered him half a dozen shorts and half a dozen summer shirts in assorted colors. With time running out, Queen Valerie ordered her dad the Handyman's complete toolbox, complete with every tool imaginable. Time was out, Queen Valerie clicked the "place order now button."

Within seconds, the UPS big brown helicopter pilot was outside Thalia's office ringing the doorbell. Once again JJ was startled. "Hello, my name is Stephen, and I have a delivery for Queen Valerie's Dad" JJ told the man in the brown uniform, Stephen, to put it in the corner next to the other packages. JJ was impressed, "maybe, just maybe I did misjudge Queen Valerie.

The third time slot was devoted to her mom. Realizing she only had 28 minutes left, Queen Valerie had to hurry, looking at her long list,

Queen Valerie began to scroll. Quickly, she placed in her virtual cart some new Rachel Ray cookware, and a new serving spoon, serving fork and a complete new set of stainless-steel knives, complete with a wooden counter knife rack. Then so Mom could be styling with Dad, Queen Valerie ordered her mom some cute summer outfits complete with a new pair of Dr. Scholl's arch supporting sandals. For a special gift, she ordered her mom a very expensive emerald necklace Time was out, Queen Valerie clicked the "place order now" button.

Within seconds, the white cargo helicopter pulled up outside. Getting out of the helicopter, was a young lady, Ella Rose, she rang Thalia's doorbell. JJ was prepared and was looking forward to seeing a package for Queen Valerie. JJ opened the office door, "Hello, my name is Ella Rose and I have a large delivery for Queen Valerie's Mom. JJ told the young lady Ella Rose, to put them with the rest of the packages. JJ was mystified, Queen Thalia was wrong about Queen Valerie. JJ had to put a stop to this whole thing before Queen Valerie was made into one of The Wishers and made to work the helium mines forever.

Queen Valerie started working on the last person, her sister Vivian. Sure, her sister was an over achiever, sure her sister was annoying, but she still loved her. Vivian was into electronics, so Valerie ordered her a new Apple laptop, a Nintendo switch and a new Apple cellphone, complete with full service for a year. Queen Valerie placed everything into the virtual cart and without a second thought clicked the "place order now" button. Time was out.

Within seconds the Target helicopter was in the driveway. JJ was curious, "Did she finally order something for herself?" Practically ripping the packages from Angelica's hands, the Target pilot, he saw the impossible, every Target had Queen Valerie's sister name on it. Frustrated, JJ told the Target pilot, Angelica to put the packages next to the many other packages in Thalia's office.

JJ thought to himself, "How does one have an unlimited shopping spree and not buy anything for herself? She bought for her dad, her mom and her sister, Vivian, and for the less fortunate students at Hallsberry School. Queen Valerie is not a bad child, she does not deserve this! What do I do?"

Mr. Dulany sat in his cell, wondering how he was going to get out this dungeon, wondering if Valerie was okay and wondering how he would explain this to Valerie's parents. They would probably get him a shirt that had "Worst Babysitter Ever" written on the front.

Having successfully maneuvered the unlimited Target shopping spree, Valerie was proud of herself. Queen Valerie stayed focused and bought for everybody on her list. Now she had 15 minutes to pack for her trip to the Philippines, this was where her dad was born and raised, this would be a family vacation to remember. Queen Valerie, with the help of Elli, went to her room and began to pack.

Urgently, JJ came running into her room. Suddenly, the cloud shook with tremendous force. This was possibly the biggest tremor today. Out of breath, JJ frantically exclaimed "I need to talk to you!"

Hyacinth Beans

Worried about Thalia's helper, JJ, Queen Valerie immediately offered him help. She ordered Juan to get JJ some water. "Please sit down, JJ." JJ drank some water and calmed himself down. "Maybe, you should sit down, Valerie" suggested JJ. Mystified, Queen Valerie asked, "Why do you call me Valerie and not Queen Valerie?"

Nervously, JJ began to spill the beans, "You are not the Queen, this is the Cloud of Thalia and Queen Thalia is in charge, the rest of us are Wishers. Wishers are children who did not appreciate what they had in life; they wanted the world given to them without working for it. Queen Thalia manipulated the children, became their friends and used them. After the children signed their legal rights away, Queen Thalia fulfills everything on their wish lists. Once the final wish is fulfilled, they become a Wisher."

Completely naïve Queen Valerie nonchalantly asked, "So why are you telling me?" Pausing for a second Queen Valerie continued packaging. "I have less than 15 minutes to pack so Thalia can grant me my final wish, I need to head the airport where my family and I will spend a week visiting the Philippines, then I will come back and where you and Thalia have both promised me my life will change forever."

"OMG!" exclaimed Queen Valerie, "now I hear it." "What's going to happen to me?" asked a very anxious Queen Valerie. "First, you are not the Queen, the only Queen on this cloud is Queen Thalia. If you go on that trip to the Philippines, once you get off the plane, your final wish is over, including no more family, and you officially become a Wisher. Queen Thalia has told me you will be at the bottom of the mine searching for helium!" JJ bashfully stated.

Valerie sighed, "I knew this was too good to be true!" Valerie started to cry. JJ walked over to comfort Valerie. "This story isn't over!" JJ exclaimed. "I know you are not a Wisher you have shown yourself to be a kind, unselfish and generous!" Still upset, Valerie asked "Why are you helping me? What are we going to do?"

"I am helping you because you made some bad decisions during the Covid-19 pandemic, you shouldn't be punished this severely. The first thing we are going to do is not get on that plane for the Philippines! If you never get on the plane, you never have to get off the plane!"

"Thank you! Thank you! Thank You!" replied Valerie as she ran over to give JJ one of her signature hugs. As she hugged JJ, a big brass key fell from her pocket. JJ heard the key fall. "Don't worry, I've got your back" as he thought about the key. JJ could not resist asking "What are you doing with this key?"

"I heard you talking to one of the guards, I believe you are holding a friend of mine in the dungeon, his name is Mr. Dulany, I go nowhere without him!" shouted out Valerie. "The unwanted guest belongs to you. This man risked his own life to try and rescue you?" exclaimed JJ. Curious, JJ told her nobody ever comes to rescue the Wishers. "He must think you are a very special" JJ stated. All Valerie said was "He does." She smiled. JJ handed the key back to Valerie.

Queen Thalia was still yelling. "No food until you find more helium. Dig faster. Dig deeper. Dig, Dig, Dig. I do not care if you are tired. I do not care if you are hungry. I do not care if you miss your families. I only care you find more helium. Dig!" Finally taking a break, Queen Thalia felt another tremor. A few more hours here and Queen Thalia needed to go back and check on her newest Wisher, Valerie.

Feeling the Cloud of Thalia sink a few more inches, JJ encouraged his new friend Valerie to get moving, Queen Thalia was eventually going to come back, and they did not want to be there when the Queen of Mean returned. Valerie was upset, she was looking forward to her trip to the Philippines, an all-expense paid vacation to a tropical paradise.

Last year in her fourth-grade class with Mrs. Armstrong, Valerie did a report for geography class about the Philippines. She learned about the capitol Manila, a bustling modern capitol, but just outside the city limits were century old churches filled with colonial history, like San Agustan Church that was built in 1589 or the church built in 1786 by the Spanish in Miago. Valerie learned about the scuba diving in Tubbataha Reef and scuba diving with the shipwreck vessels in Coron.

Valerie wanted to see it all. She reported on the Banaue Rice Terraces, the underground rivers in Puerto Princesa and the Coral Gardens in Coron. This adventurous young lady wanted to sit on the white beaches in Boracay. She wanted to take her sister Vivian swimming in the South China Sea, the Philippine Sea and the Pacific Ocean, all while sipping on peach iced tea wearing her favorite mustard yellow swimsuit.

Finally, before leaving she wanted to see the Chocolate Hills in Bohol and the Mayon Volcano in Albay, it had one of the worlds few perfect cone peaks. Mrs. Armstrong gave her A+ on her report, but this trip was not going to happen, maybe next year. Finally realizing she had nothing to grab, Valerie ran to the dungeon to rescue Mr. Dulany.

Running past Elli and Maria, JJ and Valerie ran for their lives. North, along the hallway to the stairs, down the 32 steep stairs, right at the first intersection, then another right, two lefts and a right at the gargoyle, the very ugly dirty old gargoyle. The dungeon was the 13th door on the right. Being Queen Thalia's assistant had its advantages, the biggest privilege was he could go anywhere at any time.

PART TWO

Valerie counted the doors on the right, scanning each window for any signs of Mr. Dulany. Even though the cells were empty, there was a guard by each door, they passed by Michael, Arush, Arushi, and Sherlyn. Valerie continued to count and search, 5, Maria, 6, Julian, 7, Jaiden, 8, Cristian. Frustrated, but determined, Valerie continued 9, Dayamin, 10, Julie, 11, Kaitlyn, 12, Kayden, a finally 13, Ashley. JJ ordered the guard, Ashley to move.

Seeing Mr. Dulany huddled in the corner made Valerie upset. She called out his name, "Mr. Dulany, Mr. Dulany!", but he did not answer, he was cold, hungry and mentally beaten down. Taking charge Valerie commanded JJ, "Get your keys out and open this door." JJ scrambled to find his keys, nervously he tried the first silver key, it did not work, he tried his second gold key, it didn't work, he only had one key left, the copper key, and it didn't work either.

Worried about Mr. Dulany, Valerie began to panic. Wondering what to do next, it came to her like an eagle swooping down on a rattlesnake, swoosh. She grabbed the key from her pocket and swiftly opened the lock. JJ was confused, his keys should have worked. Valerie ran into the dark musty cell to help Mr. Dulany. JJ quickly followed her into the small cell.

Suddenly Valerie heard a voice, an eerily familiar voice, it was Queen Thalia. "I wasn't sure I could trust you JJ, I knew you were weak, that's why I had the locks changed, but to help a future Wisher is unacceptable, it's intolerable, it's treason." Meanwhile, Valerie was trying to help Mr. Dulany, "It is me, your favorite neighbor, your favorite Hallsberry School student, your favorite friend. Please respond."

The Queen of Mean continued, "JJ, I never thought you would go this far. As a reward for your hard work and service for the Wishers you and your friends will be eliminated in an hour, only the rats will mourn your passing." Then Queen Thalia started to close the door to dungeon #13. Then, another tremor shook the Cloud of Thalia, the tremor was long and strong, knocking JJ down.

Green Beans

The last tremor lowered the cloud a few more inches. Queen Thalia was shaken up and dropped her keys. As Valerie talked to Mr. Dulany, he came to life, Valerie's positive attitude and beautiful smile had her a special place in his heart. Valerie was truly was an inspiration to Mr. Dulany. The tremors stopped and Queen Thalia went to pick up her keys.

Seizing the moment, Mr. Dulany surprised everyone. In one swift motion Mr. Dulany got himself up, ran past Valerie, avoided JJ, slammed the dungeon door open and flattened Queen Thalia. Do you see what a little inspiration will do? In the heat of the moment Mr. Dulany yelled "Run, Everyone, Run! Stunned, Queen Thalia laid on the ground unable to move.

Valerie, JJ and Mr. Dulany ran. They ran to the left, to the right, the guards, Maria and Elli did nothing. They ran past Arushi, Michael and Nayamarie, but the guards did nothing. The guards were Wishers too, promoted to guards only for their hard work and dedication to the Queen. New Wishers always went to the helium mines first.

The Wishers were all slaves and destined for a life of servitude because of their greed and attitude. Escaping was the only answer, escaping was impossible, the Queen was too powerful. If Valerie escaped, there was hope, hope for everyone. The trio ran up the 32 steep narrow stairs, the tremors began again almost knocking Mr. Dulany off the non-banistered slim stairway. Relentless in their attempt to escape the Cloud of Thalia, they continued running.

Queen Thalia pursued the trio of rebels. She ordered the guards Alexis, Amari and Diana to stop them. The guards ignored the Queen. Feeling betrayed, getting aggravated, and seething with frustration, the Queen ran after Valerie. As she desperately ran past Arushi, she "accidently" tripped on Arushi's foot, Queen Thalia stood up, ran past Michael and "accidently" tripped on his foot. Running past Cristian, Queen Thalia avoided Cristian's foot only to slip on a pile of Taki's that Cristian "accidently" spilled.

Almost out of the castle, Valerie needed to catch her breath. Mr. Dulany felt like he was dying, he needed a break too. Feeling guilty, Valerie asked JJ what happened to the Wishers that were left behind. "Sadly," JJ began, "because of my disloyalty and betrayal, we will be made to work longer and harder. Breadcrumbs will be our meals, rocks will become our mattresses and working an extra day will become our fun!" The cloud shook again.

Mr. Dulany wondered why the tremors were occurring. Valerie was an excellent science student she answered the question. Basically, the Cloud of Thalia is held up by helium, a byproduct of natural gas. There is no more natural gas which means no more helium, the Cloud of Thalia is sinking, sinking quickly.

"We can't leave all The Wishers behind!" Exclaimed Valerie. Worried about Queen Thalia catching up with them, he strongly encouraged Valerie to keep moving. Valerie refused to move. "It's all of us or none of us," Valerie dramatically proclaimed.

"Go home, Valerie!" encouraged JJ. "This is not your battle, every Wisher knew the consequences if we continued to act selfish, be greedy and have a bad attitude. The pain will be over soon, once the cloud loses enough helium, gravity will take over and Queen Thalia's castle will come crashing to the ground."

Valerie was horrified. Almost in tears, she was shocked that JJ would allow so many children to perish because of a mistake. "Children can change, attitudes can change, this has to change" demanded Valerie. The tremors began again, each time they got stronger and longer. Mr. Dulany insisted they leave the castle.

"Spoken like a true Queen" replied JJ. "If you let me finish, rumor is once the cloud loses enough helium, the cloud dissipates releasing everyone from the curse. Simply put, every Wisher is returned home and given a second chance. The Wishers have been working on this plan for a long time. There is plenty of helium in those mines, however we have successfully managed not to find it!"

Like a woman possessed by the devil, The Queen of Mean, Queen Thalia, came up to the courtyard where the trio of rebels were. Another tremor hit hard, knocking Mr. Dulany to the ground. Queen Thalia demanded everyone to stop. Nobody Stopped. Queen Thalia ordered the guards, Amari and Alexis to stop the criminals. Amari and Alexis did nothing.

JJ told Valerie and Mr. Dulany to go, The Wishers would be fine. JJ told them he would distract the Queen until the curse was removed. Valerie paused and said, "Thank you for being a true friend, thank you for having my back." Mr. Dulany grabbed Valerie by the hand and insisted they run, run for their lives. Another strong tremor hit, and the cloud sank again.

Queen Thalia was crazy, running hysterically towards JJ, Valerie and Mr. Dulany. Thinking they were trapped by the closed castle gates they began to slow down, when they came a little closer the guards Diana and Ahmed opened them for their immediate escape, however they also closed as soon as the two went through. Queen Thalia was out of control.

Valerie and Mr. Dulany ran towards the beanstalk. Mr. Dulany was getting tired, he instructed Valerie to go on without him. He told her slide down the beanstalk, rather than climb. Valerie grabbed the hand of Mr.

Dulany and proudly proclaimed, "No Man left behind!" They both smiled at each other and ran towards the beanstalk. Bravely, Valerie let Mr. Dulany go first, down he went, within seconds Valerie jumped onto the beanstalk and she began her swift descent back to Earth.

Valerie and Mr. Dulany both heard the tremendous explosion. As they held the beanstalk tightly the deafening noise made their ears ring. Looking up, Mr. Dulany saw the cloud dissipating and Queen Thalia's castle hurling down, he tried to slide down the beanstalk faster, but gravity works at its own speed. Mr. Dulany prayed for Valerie's safety.

Halfway down the giant bean stalk, Valerie held on for dear life. She was hurling toward Earth faster than a snow leopard chasing a lone antelope. She heard the explosion and she wondered if The Wishers were back home. Valerie saw the cloud dissipating and Queen Thalia's castle hurling down. Valerie prayed for Mr. Dulany's safety. Seeing the castle hurl faster and faster towards them Valerie began to scream, "NOOOOOOOOO OOOOOOOOOOOOOOOOOOOOOOOOOOOOOOOOOOOOOOOOOOOO OOOOOOOOOOOOOOOOOOOOOOOOOOOOOOOOOOOOOO!"

Green Bean Casserole

"Wake up. Wake up Valerie!" Mom gently demanded. "You're having a bad dream." Dripping with sweat, Valerie opened her eyes. Vivian was sitting at the end of the bed and began laughing, "she's probably dreaming of boys, that would give me nightmares!" Valerie sat up and saw Mom next to her, and Dad who was standing by the doorway.

"Where's Mr. Dulany? Is Thalia still chasing us? Is Mr. Dulany, okay? Am I okay?" frantically asked a very hysterical Valerie. Dad quickly reassured his daughter, "Mr. Dulany is doing fine, I saw him working his garden when we came home, he asked me if you wanted to help him plant some tomatoes, peppers, sunflowers and beans this afternoon.

Mom jumped into the conversation "Why would your friend Thalia be chasing you?" Vivian interrupted "ex-friend". Mom continued "You seem to be okay. What happened while we were gone?" Valerie started to ramble, "seeds, big beanstalk, Queen, the Wishers, evil, the castle". Nobody understood a word she was saying, attributing it to the dream.

Vivian ran over to Valerie tossing her a small Target bag. "Here we got this for you!" Grabbing one of Valerie's hands, Vivian was shocked, "By the look at these beautifully manicured hands you don't need it" Valerie took her hand back and opened the small bag revealing a bottle of OPI white nail polish. Vivian still impressed with the manicure, looked at her sister's foot and noticed the pedicure and asked, "Who did this?" Valerie reached over and whispered into her sister's ear and said, "Esmeralda and Ayesha."

"I'm sorry for the way I acted, Vivian I am so proud of you, Mom and Dad thank you for everything you do for Vivian and me. I Love you guys so much" Valerie said as she frantically tried to come to reality. Vivian showed Valerie a bag from Panda Express, "I'm sorry I ate all the Eggo Waffles this morning, I was being kind of bratty, it's your favorite fried calamari with guacamole and garlic mashed potatoes." Disappointed, but happy her sister thought about her, Valerie said, "Thank you" Laughing, Vivian said "It's orange chicken with half fried rice and half chow Mein."

Valerie was ecstatic. Vivian also handed Valerie a Lipton Peach Iced Tea. The two sisters hugged. As Dad watched Valerie "waking up", he went through the mail. "Vehicle sticker registration, Visa bill, Vivian looks like Evelyn is having a virtual birthday party and look Valerie you have letter from the Target corporate offices." Dad handed Vivian her birthday invitation, Mom the bills, and Valerie the letter from the Target corporate offices.

Mom was mad, "Let the girl eat, it's just mail" Valerie shoved another orange chicken in her mouth, began to chew and then grabbed the letter. "It's probably an invitation to join the exclusive Red Card club!" They love me so much they want to give me a credit card. Mom and Dad looked at each other repulsed at the thought of their ten-year old having a credit card.

After taking another bite of fried rice, Valerie frantically ripped the envelope open. Slowly, she began to read the letter from Bruce Cornwall, CEO of The Target Corporation. With sand still in her eyes, all the ten-year Valerie saw was words, a long letter with words. "What is it?" asked Vivian. Valerie handed Mom the letter.

Valerie continued to eat the chow Mein with orange chicken and with fried rice. Mom read the letter, smiling as she read. Trying to be funny

Vivian sarcastically asked "Mom's smiling, so it must be good news. Valerie is banned from Target she spends too much money there. Finally, Dad chuckled and laughed, agreeing with Vivian.

Mom started to cry, Dad started to worry, but Mom had tears of joy. Mom started to explain, "Remember when this Covid-19 pandemic started? I asked both of you girls to write letters asking for help for the community in wake of the pandemic, Vivian wrote to Santa Claus, CEO of the North Pole, and Valerie wrote to the Bruce Cornwall, CEO of the Target Corporation."

Mom continued, "Well, while Santa Claus still has not answered, the CEO of Target has. Because of your touching letter asking for help for the less fortunate at Hallsberry School and Glendale Heights, he has started the Valerie Foundation, to help feed the many families in our area, the first semi-truck of non-perishable items will arrive Monday morning at 7:00 am at Hallsberry School. It will have cereal, vegetables, pasta, pasta sauce, peanuts and macaroni and cheese. Mr. Cornwall is very proud of you, and hopes many young people follow your example and says you are an inspiration to all!

Part Three

THE
INVISIBLE
GIRL

The Unseen Answer

The Hallsberry Kingdom was behind her, the Covid-19 pandemic was behind her, Valerie was now in middle school. Sixth grade, the big school, this is where dreams are made. There was theatre, musicals, sports teams, better classes, better lunches and hopefully better friends. Valerie was growing up and things were changing. The Hallsberry Kingdom was great, but the future awaited her. The teachers were great in the Hallsberry Kingdom, but they might be great in the middle school too. She would miss Mr. Dulany at school, but she could see him anytime she wanted, they were next door neighbors.

Mr. Dulany and Valerie were neighbors for years, their friendship was very special. He helped her with her difficult homework, and she helped him around the house, mostly gardening. Mr. Dulany thought of Valerie has another daughter. He had also worked in the Hallsberry Kingdom for years and watched out for all the students, he bonded with many of them. He was a good neighbor, loved to garden, but every year his garden would get bigger and bigger, yet every year he would get older and older. Valerie liked to help him in the garden and Mr. Dulany desperately needed the help.

However, Valerie did not like getting her nails dirty. Her classic white nail polish was her signature look. But she liked the aspect of gardening, watching a seed turn into a plant and producing more vegetables was remarkable, it was the circle of life. Mr. Dulany had his massive vegetable farm in the back yard and in the front of Mr. Dulany's house he had beautiful flower display. His front yard was overflowing with marigolds, pansies, inpatients, snap dragons, lilies, roses, chrysanthemums, and tulips.

This year he tried growing giant sunflowers. He started them inside, but when he brought them outside, a creature, probably from the black lagoon ate them. In a last-ditch effort, he replanted some seeds in the garden in the backyard and protected them with chicken wire. As the sunflowers grew, he released them from the cages and gave them poles for support as they reached close to ten feet tall. Valerie loved the beautiful huge sunflowers and admired the extraordinary determination that Mr. Dulany had. Nobody or nothing was going to stop Mr. Dulany from having the biggest sunflowers in town.

But most importantly she liked helping Mr. Dulany. As they worked in natures back yard the two would talk about everything. He would never judge, never gossip but always listen and always be there to offer guidance and wisdom. He liked to share his harvest of peppers, tomatoes, cucumbers, squash, melon, onions and herbs to Valerie's family, as well as to other neighbors and friends. As Mr. Dulany's garden season was ending, Valerie's middle school year was just beginning.

For the first time in middle school history, they were having a career day for the sixth-grade students. Guest speakers from different fields would be at the middle school talking about their jobs. In approximately a week, each guest would be allowed to take one student from the kids that sign up at their career table on a one-week field trip. This professional would mentor the student for a week. It would be a week they would never forget.

On Friday, the sign-up sheets of career choices were to be posted. Over the weekend, the students were to think about their future goals, future jobs, to think about what they really wanted to do the rest of their lives. Most students thought it was a little early in life, they were only 12, to have to decide their futures. Valerie as well as the new principal, Dr. Higgenbotham, thought it was never too early to start.

During lunch period on Friday, the sheets were posted on the cafeteria wall. There was a sheet for doctors, policeman, fireman, video gamers, skateboarders, pro athletes, lawyers, nurses, fast food workers, clowns, game designers, politicians, models, actors, pop singers, and candy makers. Valerie looked at the list and only one stood out, but she wanted to think about her choice.

Over the weekend she thought about her choice, it was not a hard choice. On Saturday, she saw Mr. Dulany starting to close his garden for the season, "Need help?" she awkwardly asked. Holding his sore back while pulling out a dead tomato plant, Mr. Dulany smiled and said "Thought you would never ask. You know this garden is half yours by now. With all the work you put into it, you deserve at least half."

Valerie smiled and ran into Mr. Dulany's yard. "No, our family eats and takes from your garden, this garden belongs to you." Mr. Dulany quickly replied "There would be no garden without you! I am getting older, and my kids are not interested in my gardening, but year after year you continue to come out here and help me. Look at this garden, everything you see will be yours one day!"

Valerie was excited, even though it was the end of the season, Valerie envisioned the garden midsummer and realized that this was going to be hers one day. The big old garden in Mr. Dulany's back yard was going to be hers. The questions raced through her mind would she change the garden? What would she plant? Would she change the name? Would she do his garden justice? Would she keep his legacy alive? Sensing something was wrong she asked Mr. Dulany "Are you okay?"

Seeing a tear in Valerie's eye, Mr. Dulany assured Valerie his Parkinson's disease was not progressing. "I have always been honest with you and always will be honest with you. I am not going anywhere!" Together they continued pulling out the dead tomato, pepper and cucumber plants and putting them in the big brown garbage container. They worked hard cleaning out the buckets, so they were ready for next year's spring planting.

Valerie was usually very talkative, telling Mr. Dulany about her crushes, her friends, who did not seem to be friends and everything that was going in her life. Valerie, although was very careful in the words she chose, was always very open and honest. Mr. Dulany appreciated this about Valerie. However, he was worried about the silence, did he do or say anything wrong?

They had worked hard all morning, they were hot and sweaty, he decided to go in and get two bottles of ice-cold Lipton Peach Tea from the refrigerator. Valerie could not decide if she could ask Mr. Dulany about signing up for her career choice. She thought he was losing his gift of wisdom. Last week, he told her to ask David, her crush, out on a date. What could it hurt? All he could say was no. Valerie did.

Mr. Dulany had given the worst advice ever. Valerie was a very quiet and shy girl. Not only did David say no, but he also said "NOOOOOOOOOOOOOOOOOOOOOOOO! Not in a million years" and then laughed hysterically. David was a very popular figure at the middle school, he was a leader and athlete. Being arrogant and mean, David told everyone Valerie had a crush and him and asked him out. David embarrassed Valerie in every class. The whole sixth grade class just stared at Valerie on the bus ride home. This was the worst advice ever. Valerie asked herself "Why? Why, did I listen to that bad, bad man Mr. Dulany?

The Mysterious Response

After that bad advice, Valerie was very hesitant to ask Mr. Dulany for advice. When she told him, what had happened Mr. Dulany was heartbroken, Valerie was very smart, personable and had a heart of gold, and he knew he was biased, but she was very pretty. Mr. Dulany told Valerie David was an idiot, and one day when he "woke" up, he would regret it. Valerie smiled realizing that David was an idiot, and maybe Mr. Dulany did not give her bad advice, she decided to ask Mr. Dulany the question.

Handing Valerie an ice-cold glass, with no ice, with the bottle of the ice-cold Lipton Peach Ice-tea, Mr. Dulany looked at the quiet young lady, he asked Valerie if everything was okay. Valerie said "No." Mr. Dulany was all ears.

Valerie started to speak. She told him of the career day, the sign-up sheets and the opportunity for one individual, in each group, to spend an entire week away from school and on a field trip. An opportunity of a lifetime. Mr. Dulany was confused, he did not understand the problem.

Valerie continued, "Well you know sixth graders, most of them are immature, just want to have fun. They will sign-up for McDonald's to get free chicken nuggets and French fries, they will sign-up to be a clown just to pull pranks on everyone. Do you know how important the whoopie cushion is to a sixth-grade student? Every girl in sixth grade thinks she is a model. Do you know what Kylie Jenner has done to young ladies?"

Taking a deep breath and a large refreshing sip of the Lipton Peach Iced-Tea, Valerie paused for a moment. Then she started talking again, "The boys all think they will become professional gamers, playing Mario Carts, NBA basketball and Minecraft for money. Some people think they will become You Tube stars. And I love the ones who have already given up on their education. Their Mom and Dad think that their children are the next Aaron Rodgers, Stephen Curry or Michael Jordan."

Still confused, Mr. Dulany asked Valerie, "So, what is the problem?" Valerie quickly responded, "They think it is a joke, they are in sixth grade, they need to figure out their career path before it's too late. There are girls who think they can be actresses, there are children out there who think they can become professional skateboarders. Let's get real!"

Mr. Dulany responded to Valerie, "You are a strong independent young lady, it doesn't matter what other children do, as long as you are not hurting anyone, you do what is right for Valerie." Valerie finished filling the brown garbage can and smiled, "What happens if I am the only one?" asked Valerie. Sometimes the road less traveled is harder, but the rewards are better," said a confident Mr. Dulany.

On Monday, the signup sheets were posted in the busy cafeteria. Many of the boys flocked to the professional video game sheet, many of the girls ran to the modeling sheet only to be hit with reality when Camilla, by far the prettiest girl in the school, strolled up. Amari, the star and captain of both the football and basketball teams chiseled his way to the front of the line to spend a week with Justin Fields, quarterback for the Chicago Bears. The week-long field trip to a McDonald's was filled quickly by hungry teens.

The lunch bell rang, lunch was over, it was now or never. Valerie cleaned up her half-eaten cheeseburger and threw all her garbage into the trash.

The crowd of teens reminded Valerie of the wildebeest stampeding across the gorge in the Lion King. Mr. Dulany was right, she was independent, it didn't matter what other children did. As she threw away her garbage, she looked at the sheets, McDonald's was full, professional sports athlete was full, professional gamer was full, even the executive chocolate maker was filled with names too numerous to count.

Suddenly, the principal, Dr. Higgenbotham appeared telling Valerie, "Hurry up Sadie, lunch is over, you don't want to be late for class again. One more writeup and I will have to call your parents." Valerie was appalled, the principal didn't even know her name. Valerie looked at the sheets one last time, nobody signed up to be a doctor, a lawyer, an accountant, a nurse or even a potato farmer.

In a rush, the shy Valerie grabbed her blue Bic pen and signed her name on the nurse's sheet. As long as she could remember she wanted to be a nurse. She liked to help when her younger sister Vivian was hurt, always the eager athlete, always getting hurt. Valerie loved being the first one to get a bandage and making things better. When Mom cut herself preparing dinner, or Dad bumping his knee while cutting the grass, Valerie was always the first one on the scene with the band-aid, the bacitracin zinc ointment or the ever-popular ice pack. Valerie loved helping people. "Come on Sadie, get to class" ordered the powerful Principal, Dr. Higgenbotham.

About an hour later Camilla came and picked up the sheets, during her free period she volunteered in the front office and this brilliant move kept her informed of everything. As Camilla gathered the sheets, she noticed how Valerie was the only one to sign-up to be a nurse, "what a nerd" she snickered to herself. Camilla also saw all the girls who wanted to be models, "Like they have a chance!" Camilla arrogantly said to herself.

The loud school bell rang, finally, the day was over. Valerie got on the bus very quietly, almost like she was invisible. Valerie was hungry, she barely ate that terrible thing they call lunch, today she would try cooking pasta, probably rigatoni and bruschetta, when she got home. There was something about cooking that was soothing.

Soon afterward Camilla, the model, and Amari, the athlete, jumped onto the bus laughing and joking making enough noise for four buses. While Valerie tried to avoid trouble, she sat near the front, Camilla and Amari sat in the back, gossiping, being bullies, and doing who knew what. As long as they left Valerie alone, she didn't care what they did.

The bus engine roared, the gossiping started. The diesel engine was loud, but the 81 teens aboard the big yellow bus was louder. Soon everyone on the bus was staring and laughing at Valerie. All she heard was, "I can't believe her, what a nerd, she wants to become a nurse." Soon fingers were pointed, the kids stared at her and began to laugh all because she wanted to become a nurse.

Valerie's bus stop was here. She got off the bus quickly. The big yellow bus left, and Valerie began to cry. Walking home Valerie thought to herself "Why? Why, did I listen to that bad, bad man Mr. Dulany?"

The Obscure Choice

It was a long week, being teased by the whole sixth grade class, but Valerie made it through. She sat by herself in the lunchroom, on several days she decided to walk home to avoid the bus. The teacher's protected her in class, Valerie often sat in the front of the class claiming she could not see, where the teacher could easily watch and protect her from the bullies. Between classes she ran swiftly down the long hallways to avoid any comments or confrontations.

Friday came and the winners were announced for the career week field trips. At 3:00, Principal, Dr. Higgenbotham came on the intercom and announced the once in a lifetime field trip winner, "The McDonald's field trip is going to William, the Fannie Mae chocolate making excursion is Joseline, spending a week with Professional Gamer George Thompson is Sophia." He continued, naming many of the winners. After what seemed an eternity he came to the end of the list, "finally the weeklong career program with Justin Fields of the Chicago Bears will be the one and only star athlete himself Amari."

From class to class, down every hallway you heard the roar of excitement, Amari was getting the love and support he was getting for his athleticism. As the noise settled down, Principal Higgenbotham started to announce the winner of the coveted top model award, otherwise to most beautiful girl in the middle school, obviously Camilla. "Spending a week at Chicago's top modeling school with the number 1 model in the world, Kylie Jenner, will be.......... Valerie?" questioned the astonished principal.

The hallways were quiet, Valerie was ecstatic. The classrooms were quiet, Valerie had tears of joy in her eyes. The school was mystified, Valerie was excited. Then over the intercom, his secretary told the principal to put on his glasses. "I'm sorry," said the remorseful principal, "I read that wrong, sorry Valerie you are not the most beautiful girl in the school, that honor goes to Camilla, Valerie since you are the only one to sign up for the nurse, you get to spend a week at Parkview Hospital."

Camilla was excited, Valerie was crushed. The mean children congratulated Camilla, they laughed at Valerie. Camilla was going to spend a week modeling and wearing designer clothes, having hairstylists work her hair and having make-up artists paint her face, hopefully ending up on the cover of Vogue magazine. On the other hand, Valerie would be spending five days with the sick, hurting people in the small village of Glendale Heights.

Once again on the bus ride home the children congratulated Amari and Camilla, proud of their successful popular cool friends. Amari flexed his muscles, signed autographs and promised everyone front row seats to his first game as starting quarterback, the children were star struck. Camilla flipped her hair constantly, puckered her lips and took selfies with her friends, and promised everybody they could come to her first cover shoot party, the children were fascinated. Valerie sat alone near the bus driver, said nothing and promised nothing.

Valerie saw Mr. Dulany trimming his roses back when she came home, he saw a very sad young lady. Holding nothing back, he immediately asked "What's wrong?". Valerie said nothing, but her face said everything. Knowing the middle school was a hot bed of gossip, rumor and meanness, Mr. Dulany asked Valerie to get him the smaller set of trimmers out of the back shed, this gave him time to think.

"Thank you, Valerie" replied Mr. Dulany has Valerie handed the sharp scissors to him. Valerie was quiet, this was not like her with him. Mr. Dulany awkwardly broke the silence, "Did you know that the littlest plant often becomes the biggest plant? It's true, some plants start off big and powerful, but soon stutter, they grow too quickly. The little plants take their time, absorbing sunlight and water at their own pace. At the end of season, the little ones are the best bloomers."

Valerie was still quiet, thinking about her choice of becoming a nurse. The embarrassment of being accidently named the middle school's top model. Mr. Dulany took a swig of cold water, "Remember this rose in May? I was ready to throw it out, but you, yes you wanted to give it a chance. We watered this rose every day, we fertilized it, we gave it a trellis to grow on, and we kept the weeds out. Now look at it. It is the prettiest, most vibrant rose bush of them all."

"Next Monday I report to a week of training at Parkview Hospital. Amari will be having the time of his life in Bears training camp, Camilla will spend a week in front of a camera, William will be eating Chicken Nuggets and Big Macs, Joseline will be eating candy all week, and Sophia will be playing video games all week. I will spend a week learning what a nurse does. The lady in charge, Miss Llivia, says by the end of the week I will understand a nurse's job. Everybody else is having fun and I will be working!"

Not wanting to lecture Valerie, Mr. Dulany asked Valerie if she ever studied poetry in English class. Valerie said "Of course!" Did you hear of the poem by Robert Frost "The Road less Traveled?" Valerie couldn't remember. Mr. Dulany suggested Valerie read it and reminded her that it is okay to go a different direction than her classmates.

Valerie shrugged her shoulders and said she had to go work on her homework. She did not quite understand why Mr. Dulany was talking about driving down a different road, driver's education was not for a few years. She ran home and with each step she got madder and madder that she signed up for the nursing program. Before she opened the big white front door to her house, Valerie asked herself "Why? Why, did I listen to that bad, bad man Mr. Dulany?"

Monday

The Undisclosed Location

It was Monday morning and the little white school bus, number 381, dropped Valerie off at the front doors of Parkview Hospital. Miss Llivia was there to greet Valerie, "Welcome to Parkview nursing program. We at Parkview Hospital believe in a team approach to a patient's care. Everybody's job is important in helping a patient get healthy. All for one and one for all." Valerie was confused.

"I thought I was going to spend a week taking blood, checking temperatures, removing gall bladders, maybe do an open-heart surgery, maybe a brain surgery or two. I thought I would be checking heart rates, looking at odd rashes, helping with dog bites, you know the fun stuff!" Valerie exclaimed. "You have to go to school and be licensed to be a nurse," replied Miss Llivia.

Valerie was crushed. "This week will be an education in the hospital activities. You will work with many of the people who help the nurses and doctors. The receptionist, the head dietician, the, landscapers, the janitors and the volunteers are all are of this hospital's patient wellness plan. Today you will work with Jaz, our head receptionist" informed Miss Llivia.

Jaz walked over to Valerie and shook her hand. Valerie had a look of sadness on her face. Jaz saw the frown and assured Valerie that she would have a fun, today there was a medical convention with doctors from all over to world to discuss the recent covid-19 pandemic. Jaz handed Valerie a name tag, with her name on it and escorted her to the desk at the front of the hospital.

Together they walked over to the desk. Jaz told Valerie to put on her uniform, before she sat down, Valerie was confused. "I didn't bring a uniform!" exclaimed Valerie. Jaz said, "We are the first faces visitors see when they come to Parkview Hospital, we need to always wear a smile. Most people are coming here because they are sick, we need to be a ray of sunshine."

Valerie finally smiled, realizing how important the receptionist job was. Jaz reminded Valerie not to argue with the guests and always keep smiling. It was boring at first, very few visitors, but Valerie kept busy by organizing the desk. She saw a lunch bag with Jaz's name on it. Jaz asked Valerie to bring it to the cafeteria. Distracting Valerie, a mother came in looking for her daughter, who had a beautiful baby boy named Nolan last night, Jaz showed Valerie how to look up names on the computer to find out which room they were in. Valerie soon forgot about Jaz's lunch.

Jaz pointed to the room number on the computer and Valerie excitedly told the new grandmother "Room 457, take the elevator to the fourth floor, turn right and it will be on the left side, Congratulations!" all while smiling. Jaz who kept busy drawing unicorns between visitors was impressed.

Another man soon followed and said he had an appointment with Dr. Bardot. Dr. Bardot was going to look at his infection on his leg. The young man, named JJ, told Valerie he was trimming the lilac bushes in his front yard when he came across a wasp nest. It was small, and JJ thought nothing of it, but when he tried pulling it down, one wasp came after him and stung him in the back left lower leg.

Valerie was impressed, Jaz sat their quietly drawing unicorns while Valerie talked to JJ, "Can I see it?" she eagerly asked. Jaz quickly stood up exclaimed "Valerie!" JJ was stunned, Valerie was stunned. Jaz continued "It is not proper for the receptionist to ask the visitors to see their injuries." JJ quickly responded, "It's okay, it's gross. I am okay with Valerie wanting to see it!"

JJ awkwardly twisted his body to show Valerie the swollen leg. In a moment of anticipation, JJ gently grabbed the corner of the bandage. Valerie was excited, her first injury, she saw the swollen red inflamed bump, but what was under the Pokémon band-aid was the Kool part. "Nice band-aid" Valerie remarked. "My daughter, Braelyn, gave it to me!" said JJ as he slowly started to pull the Pokémon band-aid off.

The band-aid was pulled off. Jaz thought Valerie was going to faint, JJ thought Valerie was going to throw up, but Valerie came to life. The wound was bright red with oozing blood, you could see the pus just waiting to explode, this was going to be a gusher. Valerie came over smiling. "That is going to be quite the gusher, Dr. Bardot is going to be surprised."

Another man was waiting patiently behind JJ holding a large brown leather briefcase, he gently coughed trying to be recognized. Jaz instinctively noticed and interrupted the show and tell moment Valerie was having with JJ, "Dr. Bardot's office is on the second floor, take the elevator to the second floor, exit and turn left, her office will be at the end of the hallway. Valerie told JJ she was available to assist Dr. Bardot if necessary. JJ said, "Thank You!" and headed off to have the stinger removed.

The next well-dressed man stepped up to the desk, impatiently he stated, "Hello I am Dr. Rivers, I am hosting the conference on Covid-19 this afternoon. Where is it? How do I get there? Is it set-up? Did all the information come?" Jaz looked at Valerie and Valerie smiled back at Jaz feeling very confident. Jaz was impressed with Valerie's quick learning. Valerie whispered to Jaz, "I got this!"

Valerie walked around the large front desk and greeted Dr. Rivers, "No worries, we have been expecting you. Your meeting is in Conference room

D, it is straight down the corridor directly behind you, take the hallway down to the T and turn right, it is in the door on the left. The maintenance crew has been working on setting up the room all morning and the pamphlets, samples, clipboards, pens and promotional merchandise was picked up by Mario about an hour ago."

Dr. Rivers was mystified. All his questions were answered by Valerie, it seems Parkview Hospital was on top of the situation. Dr. Rivers was frozen with unexpected, good news. "Anything else?" asked Valerie. Dr. Rivers thought about it and bashfully asked Valerie "Where can I get a good cup of coffee?" "Best cup of coffee is the Starbucks on North Avenue, in the hospital coffee can be found in the cafeteria, lower level, take the elevator turn right and it is straight ahead, today's special is a three cheese, mozzarella, cheddar and American, sandwich served with a piping fresh bowl of fresh homemade hot tomato soup, all for $2.99."

As the very impressed Dr Rivers left the front desk he said, "Thank you, you are quite the young lady, the future generation is going to be okay if they are all like you." Dr. Rivers left and Valerie smiled. Valerie noticed a young boy doing the pee-pee dance, trying to avoid any messes, Valerie quickly hollered, "Boy's bathroom, behind the elevator, the brown door on the left." The boy quickly danced his way to the bathroom. Next came an older Latina teenage girl, Kaylee, with her mother, asking where she could find Dr. Pino's office, Valerie quickly looked at the map and told the pretty teenage girl "Dr. Pino's office is in room 399, the third floor all the way in the back of the hospital. Take this hallway on the right all the way down to the end, there is an elevator, take that elevator to the third floor, it will be the second door on the left. The teenager said, "Thank you!" and started to go down the hallway.

Still in ear's voice range, Valerie complimented Kaylee, "Your white dress is very beautiful, goes perfectly with your dark tan and raven hair."

Kaylee smiled and said, "Thank you!" and quickly walked down the hospital hallway. Jaz was truly impressed, "You are so good with people!"

Valerie continued all morning long taking care of the guests, while Jaz drew and colored her magical unicorns. Jaz went to the cafeteria to get a fresh cup of coffee and a Lipton Peach Iced-Tea for Valerie. Valerie had no guests and stacked the paper clips in the bowl and separated the blue pens from the black pens, while Jaz was gone. As Jaz returned another man holding a black computer case entered the hospitals entrance.

The man introduced himself as Detective Peter Robinson. Jaz was startled and Valerie was intrigued. Loving mysteries, Valerie was excited, "So who are we looking for?" Not waiting for an answer Valerie answered herself, "I know Mr. Jacobs in room 241, he looks devious, or Mrs. Cruz in room 458, or maybe it was that young man JJ who walked into the hospital with the infection. It might have been a wound from a fight, or possibly an attack. I know, it must be that handsome man, Mr. Hernandez in room 711!"

"Please stop!" pleaded Jaz. Detective Peter Robinson thought Valerie was cute with her vivid imagination. "Maybe a future detective?" he asked boldly. Valerie smiled and proudly answered "No, a future Nurse." Jaz quickly asked, "What can I do for you Detective?" We scheduled a police job fare here this afternoon" replied Detective Robinson. Valerie quickly looked at the schedule, "I don't see your name on the list." Jaz looked at the schedule too.

"Your name is not on the list, the only conference we have scheduled is Dr. Bardot in conference room D!" politely responded Jaz. "It was late, but I talked to a Miss Llivia, a real sweet young lady." Jaz called Llivia. Valerie kept him busy asking the Detective who he arrested lately, robbers? Thieves? Bullies? Mean middle schoolers?" The detective was amused but was relieved when Jaz got off the phone with Miss Llivia. "You're right the

Glendale Heights police department scheduled a job fare for this afternoon, Miss Llivia accidently left it off the schedule.

Jaz told Detective Robinson he would be in Conference room A this afternoon it is all set-up and ready to go. Valerie quickly pointed to the long hallway and said go down the hallway to the T and turn right, it is the door on the left." Jaz corrected Valerie, "No that is the directions for Conference room D, Conference room A is you take the hallway to the T and turn left, and it is the door on the right." Valerie replied, you're right, then left, not left then right."

Detective Robinson turned to his right, not Valerie's right and headed down the hallway praying he was heading in the right direction. Suddenly he stopped wondering if Jaz had meant her left, or his right or her right and his left. Confused and bewildered he was afraid to go back and ask. Meanwhile Jaz said she was going to the cafeteria to get her lunch. Surprisingly, Valerie pulled out a brown paper bag with Jaz's name on it. It was her lunch. "Sorry I forgot to bring it to the cafeteria" apologized Valerie.

Mystified, Valerie asked Jaz why she was eating her lunch here. Jaz replied, "We don't have enough help so I always eat my lunch here, so I can take care of the guests." Valerie was sad but promised Jaz could eat her lunch while she took care of all the guests. Jaz smiled and began to unpack her lunch.

Valerie noticed Jaz unpackaging her lunch. Jaz had a carton of chocolate milk, a chicken salad sandwich on whole wheat toast, a small carton of potato salad, broccoli covered in cheese sauce and a piece of French silk pie. Valerie was only 12 but should knew about proper food storage, bashfully she asked Jaz, "shouldn't that have been refrigerated? Should you be eating that?" Jaz said it was going to be okay without refrigeration. Then she dug into her lunch.

Valerie wondered how Jaz enjoyed her lunch, she was eating so fast. How did she taste all the fine flavors? Cooking was an art. Like a piece of artwork, food needed to be savored and enjoyed, not shoved in your mouth like a pig eating at the trough. Valerie looked away and helped the older lady to the elevator in search of Dr. Lively. She helped the young mother with triplets to the pediatrician on the fifth floor. Valerie called Mario to help the Detective put up some tables and banners for the job applicants. Valerie liked the slow steady rhythm of people coming, it was not overwhelming, and the time went quickly.

Suddenly, Jaz's stomach started rumbling. It was the boisterous noise heard throughout the hospital. Valerie thought she felt the ground tremble. Jaz held her stomach and put her head on the desk for a minute. Jaz began to sweat, and the terrifying noise coming from her stomach began again. Valerie was scared. Jaz covered her mouth afraid of what was to come. Valerie asked, "Are you okay?" Jaz uncovered her mouth, sat up and assured Valerie she was fine, just a little indigestion.

Valerie went back to helping the guests one at a time. Like a bolt of lightning, Jaz jumped up and swiftly ran to the bathroom. Valerie confident in her abilities to take care of the guests, sat in Jaz's executive swivel chair, then she saw the crowd starting to walk through the hospital vestibule. Valerie started to sweat.

"Where is the Glendale Heights police job recruitment office?" asked the first lady. "Down the Hall to the left and first door on the right. "Where is Dr. Pino's office?" asked the second man. The line was beginning to multiply faster than rabbits in the springtime. "Down the hallway take the elevator up to the fifth floor, room 299." "Where is Mr. Hernandez's room? Asked a young lady named Vivian." "Behind the elevator, the first door on the left," replied an overwhelmed Valerie.

The line continued to increase as Valerie did her best without Jaz. "Where is the cafeteria?", asked a hungry visitor. A very stressed Valerie answered, "Room 711". Another elderly gentleman came and asked where he could find his newest grandson, William Randolph III. Valerie answered, "lower level, first door on the right." Jaz had not returned, and the line continued to grow.

Overwhelmed and frustrated, Valerie forgot to smile. She sent parents and grandparents to the police job fair, she sent sick people to the cafeteria, Valerie sent hungry visitors to the nursery where babies were being brought into the world. She sent newspaper reporters to the bathroom. People looking to use the bathroom were sent to the lecture on Covid-19. Mrs. Cruz in room 458 was visited by people looking to attend the lecture on Covid-19. Mr. Jacobs was visited by people trying to apply for a job with the Glendale Heights police department. The small hospital began to fill with lost visitors.

As Valerie continued to instruct people where to go, the line slowly diminished. Grandparents were sent for a police department interview. Dr. Bardot's patients were sent to the cafeteria. Dr. River's patients were sent to the bathroom. Valerie was impressed with herself. She looked up at her last guest. It was Miss Llivia. Her question was "Where was Jaz?" Miss Llivia did not smile. Valerie did not smile.

Without thinking Valerie answered, "Room 911?" Feeling better, Jaz finally returned from the washroom not realizing what had happened. Miss Llivia sent Valerie to her office for a talk. Jaz sat down and redirected everyone who came back for the proper directions. Jaz apologized to everyone, taking the blame for the inexperienced helper. Jaz laughed, the visitors laughed, Miss Llivia did not laugh.

Valerie went to Miss Llivia's office and sat, waiting for Miss Llivia. Miss Llivia stayed and help Jaz redirect the visitors to their proper destinations. Valerie sat and worried, Valerie sat and sweated, Valerie sat and was scared about her future. Finally, very calmly Miss Llivia came in and just stared at Valerie, thinking about what to say to the young vulnerable girl.

"You came in today thinking that a receptionist was an easy unimportant job in a hospitable. Hopefully, you will learn from this experience, you should have called for help. WE ARE A TEAM," said a very calm Miss Llivia. "I have called the school, you can go home early today, the bus will be here soon. Abigail will drive you home. See you tomorrow, where you can report to me for a day in the cafeteria."

Valerie was upset. The bus had picked her up from the hospital and dropped her off right on her driveway on Terry Road. Mr. Dulany was out raking the leaves. He asked, "How did it go today?" "Terrible!" she screamed and continued up her driveway. Mr. Dulany replied, "Keep trying! Failures increase the probability of success!" Valerie heard him but ignored him. She ran into her house and ran into her bedroom crying and yelling, "Why? Why, did I listen to that bad, bad man Mr. Dulany?"

Tuesday

The Covert War

Today was a new day, it was Tuesday, Valerie had a new chance of showing the world she was determined to be a nurse. "What did Mr. Dulany say?" she asked herself. "Of course! He said Keep trying, failures increase the probability of success." Today Miss Llivia told her she was going to be in food service, working in the cafeteria. With a sparkle in her eye, a smile on her face and plenty of hope in her heart, she continued to get dressed.

Valerie wondered how she should dress for her work in the cafeteria. She loved cooking pasta and other small meals for her family, so this should be a fun easy day. First, she picked a cute red dress, too little girl, then her fancy navy-blue dress but Valerie thought that was too much. She went through most of her closest not able to find the right outfit. Then she heard her mother yell, "el bus esta aqui", the bus is here. Valerie quickly decided to go with her casual look, blue jeans and a nice emerald, green blouse.

"Apurte Valerie!" cried her mother. Valerie came running down the stairs, kissed her mother and ran out the door to the special Parkview Hospital bus. It was a short ride to the hospital, just a few blocks away, but Valerie thought it was special that they sent a bus just for her. For an entire week she did not have to spend a week listening to Amari, a legend in his own mind and she did not have to look at the picture-perfect Camilla.

Valerie imagined herself a princess being driven to the ball in her private carriage. Life was grand.

The bus driver, Abigail drove carefully down the streets of Glendale Heights. However, she arrived quickly at the front door to the hospital. Abigail opened the side door and told Valerie "Que tengas un buen dia, have a good day in English." Valerie replied, "Mucho Gracias" and headed to the front door where Miss Llivia was standing. Abigail and her little bus pulled away from the hospital.

"Good morning, Valerie!" said an enthusiastic Miss Llivia. In her mind Valerie said to herself, "After yesterday she should be mad at me with all the confusion, all the mayhem and all the misdirected people I caused. Why isn't she mad at me? She is such a sweet lady." Miss Llivia escorted Valerie to the lower level to meet Elena, the manager of the cafeteria.

It took Miss Llivia a few minutes to find Elena in the kitchen. Between the clouds of steam, between the ovens and grills and between all the pots and pans stood a lady stirring a large boiling pot of cinnamon raisin oatmeal. "Ashley start toasting the wheat bread, Ivy, start another pot of coffee, Theresa make sure the dishes and utensils are ready. Theresa where are the sliced strawberries?" Elena commanded.

Miss Llivia finally caught up with Elena, "This is a future nurse, please give her an experience she will not forget!" Elena looked at Valerie's name badge, "So they call you Valerie?" Valerie shook her head yes. "We need to get you a uniform." Stated Elena. "Ashley, can you get Valerie a kitchen uniform?" Valerie smiled and said she had her uniform.

Elena sarcastically told Miss Llivia "Thanks for the project!" Miss Llivia left for her office and Elena told Valerie she needed more than a smile to work in the kitchen. "First you need to clean your hands, second you need to wear this hairnet all day long", Valerie just stared at the hairnet. "And third you need to wear this apron." Valerie stared at the apron. Elena encouraged Valerie to put on the hairnet and the apron. Valerie just stood there with a tear in her eye.

PART THREE

Sensing that this was a fashion emergency for Valerie, Elena told Valerie "Look at all these gorgeous super models here, there's Ashley, Leah, Theresa and Ivy. We have to hide our beauty with these hairnets and aprons, otherwise we wouldn't get any work done around here." Valerie chuckled and put the hairnet on, cringing all the way, then she slipped on the sterile white apron tying it around her small waist four times.

"You look fabulous!" Elena announced. "I am glad you chose to put them on voluntary, otherwise I would have had to pull out the sanitation handbook and read page 3, chapter 5, section 21, paragraph 8, line 22." Valerie rudely interrupted, "Page 3, chapter 5, section 21, paragraph 8, line 22 of the Dupage County sanitation handbook clearly states anyone who works in a kitchen must wear a hairnet and an apron!" Elena was mystified but was very impressed with Valerie's knowledge of the sanitation handbook.

Valerie your training will start with making sure the dining room is ready for the breakfast rush, why don't you work with Ashley to prepare the dining room, please make sure it is clean and ready for the guests.

Ashley walked out to the dining room. Together Ashley and Valerie cleaned and sanitized each table, they swept the floor, together they positioned each chair. Ashley let Valerie fill each salt and pepper shaker and fill the napkin dispenser at each table. Valerie made coffee many times for her parents, so Ashley let Valerie make the coffee. Valerie was doing a great job and Valerie began to think maybe Mr. Dulany was right.

After finishing their first job so well, Ashley brought Valerie back to the kitchen to see Elena. Elena was impressed with Valerie, she was a hard worker, attentive and very respectable. When Valerie saw Elena she asked, "do we get to cook yet?". Elena bashfully asked, "So, you like to cook?" Valerie shook her head. Elena thought for a minute.

"Crystal, called in sick this morning. We need a toaster girl. Today we have the blueberry pancake special for $2.99, it includes all-you-can-eat pancakes, sausage or bacon, and toast. Yesterday we were swamped. Yesterday the receptionist accidently sent down a lot of people, they smelled the pancakes and stayed for breakfast. Quite the mistake but quite the day. I told Jaz to send people down again" stated Elena. Valerie was embarrassed and shrank to hide in the corner.

Elena continued, "If we put Theresa and Ivy and Leah on pancakes through the rush, we can put Valerie on the toast." "Great idea!" said Leah. "But can she handle it?" inquired Ivy. Valerie was insulted, she had cooked pasta, cheeseburgers and pot roast for her family, toast was a no brainer. Valerie stepped up and proudly announced "I accept the challenge!"

The hungry breakfast crowd was due any minute, they had only a few minutes to train Valerie. Valerie was a smart young lady. Ivy showed Valerie where the bread was, Leah showed Valerie where the toasters were, and Theresa showed Valerie where the platters were to put the toast on. "Keep toasting, until we tell you to stop!" Ashley reminded Valerie.

Suddenly, the cafeteria door opened, and the hungry crowd began to appear. "Battle stations everyone!" commanded Elena. Ashley took position at the register, Elena bunkered down at the sausage and bacon station and the heavy hitters Theresa, Ivy and Leah took their position making blueberry pancakes. Proudly, Valerie took her post on the toasters and began loading the toaster.

Ashley kept the line moving smoothly. Elena kept the sausages cooked to perfection and the applewood bacon crispy, both full in the serving pan. Theresa, Ivy and Leah kept the golden-brown pancakes loaded with fresh Wisconsin blueberries fully stocked on the warming tables. The rookie, Valerie, kept the toast popping all during the breakfast rush. She had timed it perfectly, the wheat toast alternated popping with the white toast, leaving Valerie just enough time to slice the bread in half and plate it.

Valerie never saw who kept taking the huge plates of toast that she made, she concentrated on making the toast, slice after slice, plate after plate Valerie was making the toast. Pop, slice, plate, pop, slice, plate, Valerie was a well-oiled toasting machine. Focused and motivated Valerie never noticed the plates of toast that were stacking up. Pop, slice, plate, pop, slice, plate.

The breakfast rush was over, Elena and her tired crew Ashley, Theresa, Ivy and Leah sat down among the cafeteria mess and enjoyed a cup of coffee, celebrating a successful breakfast rush. Elena told her crew what a wonderful job each one did. Ashley talked about the never-ending line, Elena thought she broke a record for most sausages cooked in a breakfast rush and Theresa bragged about her flipping skills. Ivy was amazed how sweet the blueberries made the pancakes. Lucy was astonished at Valerie's ability to keep up with the demand.

Like a bolt of lightning, it hit them at the same time. In a synchronized voice, they all screamed "Valerie!" and ran to the kitchen to see Valerie stacking another plate of toast. Snickering, Elena told Valerie that breakfast was over, and she could stop making the toast. Valerie was embarrassed, Valerie was ashamed, and Valerie wondered why everything kept going wrong in her life.

Elena saw Valerie's big brown eyes begin to tear. "It's all our fault honey, we told you to keep going until we said stop and that's exactly what you did." Valerie stood proudly and asked, "what's next". Elena wiped the tear rolling down Valerie's cheek and replied, "We need to start lunch!"

"Ashley and Valerie why don't you clean in here together, "suggested Elena. Valerie looked around the cafeteria, the same one she cleaned just a few-hours prior. "What in the world happened in here, World War 3?" she rudely asked. Ivy responded "$2.99 all you can eat pancakes! Just wait to after the $2.99 cheeseburger special, we are having for lunch. It includes a 32oz. Pepsi, a quarter pound cheeseburger and a large carton of fries. You haven't seen anything yet!" Valerie was scared.

While most of the kitchen staff scurried off to start preparing lunch, Ashley and Valerie stayed behind and cleaned the mess that was left over from the breakfast rush. They scraped butter from the chairs, picked-up runaway blueberries, collected loose creamer cups and sugar packets and scraped hardened maple syrup from the tables. It was hard work, but Valerie never complained and did an excellent job of cleaning what was left from the war.

With Crystal absent today, it was decided by Elena it would be best if Valerie stayed in the forefront of the cafeteria. With Jaz now sending the visitors to the cafeteria, business was booming and with the $2.99 cheeseburger special today should be no different. Elena had it all figured out, Ashley would work the cash register, Theresa and Ivy would grill the cheeseburgers and Elena and Leah would make the fries. Elena told Valerie her job would be to try and keep the seating area clean.

Valerie was disappointed, she knew how to cook, she loved to cook, but she was not cooking. Elena explained to Valerie that her job was to clean the table after each guest left. Valerie thought it was a pretty- simple job, throw away the trash, wipe and sanitize the table and chairs and sweep the floor. How hard could it be? Soon she would find out.

The lunch rush started out slowly, doctors came and talked about their busy afternoon schedules, Dr. Rudgers had a broken leg to mend, Dr. Cruz had to pop a pimple the size of Texas, Valerie was intrigued. Salesmen selling prescription drugs to the hospital came, Mr. Quinten sold lisinopril, a blood pressure medicine the doctors used at the hospital. Even Mr. Hernandez who was in room 711 yesterday came down to get a cheeseburger. They came, ate lunch and Valerie cleaned their tables.

Everyone enjoyed the delicious cheeseburgers, Elena's mother's secret recipe, and soon word spread. The cafeteria was packed and the line out the door was ridiculous. Nurses came in wearing their blue scrubs, Valerie was jealous, she wished she had the time to talk to them, but she was too busy cleaning tables. She worked hard trying to keep up with picking up the used plates, cups and napkins.

Grandparents came in bragging about their grandchildren. Mr. Jackson told everyone that his new grandson, Percy, looked just like him, Mrs. Avery bragged about how adorable her new granddaughter was, Mr. Avery thought he was being funny when he told Mrs. Avery, "Thank goodness, little Jasmin looks nothing like you!" Mrs. Avery did not think that grandpa was funny. They all thought the nurses did a wonderful job helping their daughters deliver the adorable babies. Valerie was jealous.

The crowd continued to stream into the cafeteria. Valerie thought to herself, "Why can't people clean up after themselves, at home my parents expect me to clean up after myself!" Valerie hustled and bustled, but she was falling behind. She thought about asking for help, but everyone was busy, Ashley never looked up helping everyone get their cheeseburgers. She saw Leah and Elena trying desperately to keep the golden fries full. Ivy and Theresa were busy flipping the burgers. Everybody's job was an important job.

A younger lady with four kids sat at the corner table. The young lady had a baby in her car seat, what seemed like a two-year cute little dark hair girl named Angelica sitting next to her eating pretzels, Valerie thought she was adorable. Across from the young mother sat two blonde boys. Valerie thought they were around five years old. Even though Valerie was extremely busy, she loved children and children usually loved her, there was something very sweet about Valerie.

As Valerie walked near the boys, she asked the bigger one "What's your name?" The boy looked like he was going to punch her. Valerie looked at the smaller boy and asked, "Are you boys twins? What's your name?" Both boys just stared at her and snarled. Valerie was not amused and continued working. After a few minutes she came back to sweep the floor, she swept up two napkins from underneath the boys and moved on to the next table.

In the corner of her eyes Valerie saw the boys throw down several more napkins. Valerie was working hard trying to keep the cafeteria clean and these two blonde bombshells were not helping. Valerie went up to the bigger boy and asked what his name was. He refused to answer. Valerie looked sternly at the younger boy and asked what his name was. The mother was oblivious to the whole situation. Valerie was getting mad. The smaller boy looked at the bigger boy and the bigger boy looked at the smaller boy.

It was like somebody scored a goal in a soccer match, the boys started screaming 'Stranger danger, Stranger Danger!" loud and proud. The cafeteria became eerily quiet for a second. The boy's mother scolded Stephen and Sammy, and they quickly apologized to Valerie. The cafeteria went back to normal. Valerie continued wiping tables and picking up garbage. Valerie found a pineapple core on a table, quite unusual considering the cafeteria did not serve pineapples.

Valerie smelled it first, but she thought it was either Stephen or Sammy. Although Valerie did not have a brother, Valerie knew boys. In Kindergarten they liked to fart, in first grade they like to fart, in second grade they like to fart, in third grade they like to fart, although a bit bashful about it in fourth grade they still liked to fart, in fifth grade the louder the fart, the prouder they were. Who knows what sixth grade would bring? And even worse what will the future bring? But it turns out the smell was coming from the baby.

The Mother got up to take the baby to the changing room in the bathroom. Valerie watched as the mother asked Stephen to watch his younger sister Angelica and his younger brother Sammy while she was changing the baby. Stephen said he would try if she promised to buy him a Reese's pieces blizzard from Dairy Queen on the way home. She answered, "Only if you do a good Job!" the mother left.

As the mother left the cafeteria, she asked Valerie where the bathroom was, Valerie quickly answered "On every floor, the bathrooms are behind the elevator, boys on the left, girls are on the right." Valerie very proud she was able to give the correct answer went back to work cleaning the coffee and Pepsi cups off some of tables. Valerie wondered how long this lunch was going to last.

She heard Stephen yelling at Sammy. Valerie heard Angelica crying because the two boys were fighting so loud. Being an experienced baby-sitter, Valerie knew she had to stop the boys from fighting, she walked over to Sammy and told him to stop fighting. She told Stephen to quit yelling at Sammy and eat his food. All Sammy heard was food and fight. Like a bomb heard around the cafeteria, Sammy yelled "Food Fight!" and threw his half-eaten cheeseburger with ketchup only at Stephen, hitting him squarely in the face. The ketchup rolled down Stephen's face like blood.

This set off a catastrophic series of events. Valerie watched as the mayhem unfolded. The two electricians eating threw their full cups of ice –cold Pepsi across the busy cafeteria where they splattered Pepsi all over a table of pediatric nurses. Several unshaven tired young doctors heard the battle cry and started squirting ketchup across the room hitting several grandparents. Finally having some fun, Grandpa Jiggets started throwing French Fry bombs from under the table.

A group of pharmacists, who took lunch at the same time every day was being attacked with an endless supply of sesame seed buns. Valerie stood there in shock. George, the head pharmacist grabbed a handful of onions from his cheeseburger, ran across the room, yelling "Food Fight!". He was hit repeatedly with tomato slices as he tried to save his secretary, Aliyah. He was pronounced stale.

The cafeteria was being destroyed. Taking cover under their table, Sammy and Stephen picked up bits and pieces of hamburger meat and tossed them high into the air, landing on innocent bystanders. The war was merciless. A mustard river ran down the middle of the cafeteria, a mountain of fries piled up in the corner, empty plates were scattered across the floor. Suddenly Elena came out of the kitchen and whistled loudly twice.

Everybody froze. Elena was mystified. Ashley was shocked. Stephen chuckled. Angelica kept crying. Sammy was scared. The mother was infuriated, she knew who started this. Doctors were cheerful, nurses laughed, and the pharmacists all apologized. Businessmen were ashamed. Grandfathers had a blast. Grandmothers looked forward to grounding the grandfathers when they got home. Valerie was ashamed of what had happened.

Unexpectantly Miss Llivia walked into the cafeteria, hungry and hopeful she would get a $2.99 cheeseburger special. Elena politely told everyone, lunch was over and asked everyone to leave. Quickly and quietly the packed cafeteria left, only Miss Llivia, Elena and Valerie were in the battle zone. Very seriously, Miss Llivia ordered her cheeseburger to go and told Valerie to meet her in her office when she was done cleaning the cafeteria. Miss Llivia left. Valerie was scared.

It was getting late, but Valerie did as she was told and cleaned the trashed cafeteria. Elena helped soak up the lakes of ketchup and mustard, Ashley scooped up the loose hamburger buns, Leah cleaned the walls, Ivy scraped the tables clean, Theresa mopped the floors. Working together, the cafeteria was cleaned and sanitized in less than an hour. Valerie took off her hairnet and soiled apron and reluctantly headed for Miss Llivia's office.

Walking down the hallway, Valerie knew she failed again, she envisioned Amari throwing a football down the field in Soldier Field with Justin Fields, having the time of his life. Camilla was probably in front of a camera smiling with a designer outfit on. Jealous was not the word.

Valerie knew she only had a few minutes before Abigail was scheduled to pick her up. Valerie, ashamed and embarrassed walked into Miss Llivia's office with her head down and sat down across from Miss Llivia who was still eating her lunch, the $2.99 cheeseburger special. "Let me start by saying tomorrow you will be outside working landscaping with Esmeralda, our head groundskeeper. Then about today," Valerie couldn't hold it in anymore, she started to cry and ran out of the room. Valerie ran straight to the little white bus where Abigail was there to take her home.

Abigail didn't even turn on the radio. She didn't know what happened, but she did know that Valerie was not happy, the ride home was silent. She brought Valerie to her driveway on Terry Road and opened the bus door. Silently she removed herself from the bus. Mr. Dulany was outside watering his eight-foot sunflowers, he saw the sad look on Valerie's face, but he was determined to make Valerie laugh. "Did you know Thomas Edison once said, "I have not failed, but I have found 10,000 ways that won't work"."

Valerie was miserable. She heard Mr. Dulany but ignored him. Mr. Dulany went back to watering his giant sunflowers, unphased at Valerie's attitude, after all she was a teenager. Valerie rushed into her house, ran into her bedroom and cried, yelling "Why? Why, did I listen to that bad, bad man Mr. Dulany?"

Wednesday

The Concealed Wrench

Today was a new day, after crying herself to sleep, she thought about what Mr. Dulany had said, "I have not failed but have found 10,000 ways that don't work. Valerie realized that she didn't fail, she just found another way that didn't work. Trying to keep a positive attitude Valerie put on a smile and tried to figure out which outfit to wear for landscaping duty. This should be an easy day I have been landscaping with Mr. Dulany for years. He is always happy with my work he never complains or yells at me when I work with him. Together, we have planted vegetables, and many flowers, he has taught me how to water, maintain and harvest the tomatoes and peppers and the roses, marigolds and lilies. Today will be an awesome day.

Valerie decided on a nice casual outfit for working outside. It was early October so the mornings were cool, and the days were warm, so a nice pair of work jeans and a t-shirt, with an old sweatshirt would work. Valerie looked down at her hands, the beautiful manicure with the classic white nail polish, she always wore gloves when she helped Mr. Dulany with his landscaping. Where were her gloves? She quickly answered herself, "In the shed, Mr. Dulany always keeps them in his shed."

Abigail and her little white bus would be here soon. Valerie threw on her jeans, her blue middle school t-shirt and the raggedy old red sweatshirt, she laced up her old red sneakers and ran to Mr. Dulany's shed. The grey and white wooden shed was huge compared to Valerie. The bus was here, Abigail waited a few seconds, then she hit the horn, beep! Beep! Beep! Valerie scrambled to find the gloves.

In the center of the shed, was the lawnmower. She quickly scanned the storage shed for the gloves, on the right was camping gear, in the back of the shed was an assortment of shovels, rakes, garden hoses, old planters and leftover garden accessories. Valerie heard Abigail beeping again, on the left was citronella candles, two gas cans, small shovels and thankfully the small yellow work gloves.

Thinking Valerie had quit the program, Abigail closed the bus door. She was sad for Valerie, years ago she went to Hallsberry School, and she too knew Mr. Dulany. College was hard, Abigail found little time for class, studying, sleep and her part-time job, but she always remembered the two rules that Mr. Dulany had taught her, #1 rule - Never Quit, #2 rule - Always remember rule #1. Abigail always remembered this and never quit college. She was scheduled to graduate this June with a Bachelor of Arts in Nursing from the University of Illinois.

Valerie tried closing the shed, but she couldn't quite maneuver the bent handle. Abigail wiped her red eyes and put the little bus in drive, hoping for a miracle, she looked up the driveway one last time and only saw a furry squirrel running up a tree, no Valerie. Meanwhile, Valerie was running from Mr. Dulany's backyard, hoping Abigail was patient. Checking both her mirrors, Abigail looked forward and gently put her foot on the gas pedal.

Bam! Bam! Bam! Abigail thought she clipped the Ford Taurus in front of her, but it was Valerie banging on the side door. "Please let me in, I'm sorry I'm late" exclaimed Valerie. "I thought you quit" replied Abigail. Valerie looked at Abigail and told her "I live by two rules #1 - Never Quit and rule #2 - Always remember rule #1, Abigail smiled as Valerie took her seat on the bus. Abigail knew Mr. Dulany was still helping the kids at Hallsberry School.

Tightly holding her small yellow gloves, Valerie stepped off the bus. Where was Miss Llivia? Miss Llivia was always here. Within seconds a young lady wearing a green jumpsuit appeared, her name tag read Esmeralda. "Hi Valerie?" asked the young lady. Valerie extended her hand to shake Esmeralda's. "I am Esmeralda, head grounds keeper for the hospital. Miss Llivia said you would be working with us today."

"Who is us?" asked a confused Valerie. Like a theatrical production another young lady wearing a green jumpsuit appeared from nowhere. "This is Aisha, my good friend and side-kick, we are responsible for keeping the lawn and flowers aesthetically beautiful for the hospital. It's important that people who come to the hospital see the beautiful flowers, it calms them and makes them feel better"

Valerie never realized or thought about the outside of the hospital, landscaping was an important part of a hospital and patient's care. Valerie bashfully asked, "So what are we going to do today? Plant flowers, trim the bushes, cut the grass?" Esmeralda and Aisha laughed. "Oh, no!" exclaimed Aisha. "In the back of the hospital is a huge pile of mulch, we will spend the entire day, moving the mulch in wheel barrels. The wheel barrels hold about 400 pounds each so it shouldn't take more than 7 or 8 hours."

Never backing down from hard work or a challenge, Valerie started to walk around the back of the hospital. Laughing hysterically Esmeralda told Valerie they were only kidding. Aisha gave Esmeralda a high five. Valerie was not impressed with their humor. As Valerie came back to the front of the hospital, Esmeralda told Valerie today they were going to plant fall bulbs for blooming in the spring. Valerie was excited she had planted bulbs up and down the sides of Mr. Dulany's driveway as well as in front of her house. Every year they planted a few more to make a bigger bolder flower showcase. In the spring the assorted tulips blossomed fiercely helping the neighbors on Terry Road get rid of the winter doldrums.

Aisha handed Valerie a small shovel to start digging. Esmeralda instructed Valerie dig a small hole big enough for the bulb, stick the bulb in and cover it up. Esmeralda asked Valerie "Got it?" Valerie decided not to be arrogant and just tell Esmeralda, "No worries, of course!" Valerie continued to plant the bulbs easily. Aisha noticed how well Valerie was doing, "If I didn't know better, I would think you had done this before."

Esmeralda mentioned to Valerie and Aisha that she was going in for coffee in the cafeteria and wondered if either one wanted a coffee. Aisha asked for a medium cappuccino with a hint of mint and Valerie told her she did not drink coffee because it stunts your growth and puts hair on your chest. Esmeralda chuckled and said, "That explains so much!"

Together Aisha and Valerie planted some of the assorted bulbs. Esmeralda came back with the medium cappuccino for Aisha and with an ice-cold water for Valerie. "I am disappointed with you girls you didn't get very far!" Valerie hesitated for a moment she did not want to be rude.

Politely Valerie began to speak, "Have you ever planted fall bulbs before?" Esmeralda surprisingly told Valerie no. Valerie explained to Aisha and Esmeralda that she has done it before, "This ground is too hard, we need to loosen it up first. We have tulip, daffodil, crocus and scilla bulbs, for better success they need to be kept together in groups. After we dig a hole about six inches deep, we need to add peat moss and make sure the roots are down in the soil, then cover it with soil" Valerie took a small sip of the cold water.

"Why are you planting bulbs so early?" Esmeralda shrugged her shoulders. Valerie continued, "The squirrels will dig half of these up, they are building their food supplies for the winter, wait about two weeks and they will almost be done. If you cannot wait, after we plant you need to sprinkle some red pepper flakes on the top of the soil, squirrels don't like the smell of the peppers."

Aisha and Esmeralda were shocked yet impressed with Valerie's knowledge of bulbs. "Where did you learn this from?" Valerie smiled and said, "A very wise man, my neighbor, Mr. Dulany." Together, Esmeralda, Aisha and Valerie continued planting the bulbs the correct way in front of the hospital. It took them several hours, but the tulips, daffodils, crocus and scilla bulbs were planted properly. Aisha hooked up the hose and started watering the planted bulbs.

Valerie was getting hungry it was lunch time and her stomach was calling her out. Esmeralda heard Valerie's stomach and offered to take Aisha and her for lunch at the cafeteria, today was a $2.99 pizza slice and Pepsi special. Valerie loved her pineapple and pepperoni pizza. The three hungry gardeners were excited for lunch, so they watered the bulbs quickly. Satisfied with the watering, Esmeralda started putting away the tools, Aisha put away the hose and Valerie was told to turn off the water.

Once again, the cafeteria was packed. Valerie hoped no one recognized her from yesterday's big debacle. Wisely, Valerie asked Aisha to get her a pineapple and pepperoni pizza slice and a peach iced tea, she would commandeer a table in the corner, where she could hide. This theory did not work, Jaz came in and said hello, Ashley saw her and said hello, Elena came over asked how she was doing and the patient from room 711, Mr. Hernandez recognized her and told her, "I brought a bag of marshmallows, just in case it happens again." He never had so much fun. Embarrassed, Valerie sunk in her vinyl chair trying to hide.

Soon Aisha and Esmeralda came back from the long line thankful Valerie was smart enough to think ahead and save a table. Aisha handed Valerie a peach iced tea, Esmeralda a large Pepsi and Aisha kept the Mountain Dew for herself. Esmeralda handed Aisha a large slice of sausage, green pepper and onion pizza, Valerie a large slice of pineapple and pepperoni pizza, Esmeralda kept the deluxe pizza to herself. This monstrosity had sausage, pepperoni, ham, onion, peppers, mushrooms and anchovies as toppings. Valerie wanted to throw up.

The three ladies joked and laughed all through lunch. Esmeralda and Aisha thought that this afternoon they should drive through the hospital grounds on the golf cart, hoping that Valerie would share some of the knowledge she had regarding plants. Valerie was finally excited, today was a great day. Esmeralda finished eating and wiped her mouth with several of the red napkins, Aisha wiped her hands and the two landscapers got up and started to walk away. Aisha mentioned a puddle of water on the floor.

Valerie noticed neither one took the time to gather their garbage and throw it in the garbage. Having empathy for the poor individual cleaning the cafeteria, Valerie picked up the garbage from her table and threw it in the garbage can, where she also stepped in some water. Noticing other tables with leftover trash on them, Valerie quickly picked up the leftover, plates, cups and napkins and tossed them in the trash.

As Esmeralda and Aisha left the cafeteria on the lower level, they noticed a small river coming from the stairway. The small river slowly became bigger and started flooding the cafeteria. Esmeralda looked at Aisha and hysterically asked, "Did you tell Valerie to use the wrench to turn the water off?" Aisha looked at Esmeralda and hysterically asked, "Did you tell Valerie to use the wrench to turn the water off?" Confused, Valerie asked, "What wrench?"

The rushing water was quickly filling the hospital cafeteria, hungry visitors began to panic and leave their lunches searching for higher ground. Esmeralda ran to get the wrench Aisha ran to get buckets and Valerie ran to get mops. Esmeralda turned off the water with the wrench. All afternoon Aisha, Esmeralda and Valerie, helped Mario mop the lower level of the hospital.

Valerie was very respectful, but she was mad. Mad that this beautiful day turned out this way, Mad at not being told about a wrench, mad about the mess, mad at Mr. Dulany. As Valerie mopped the hallway, she saw Miss Llivia standing in one of the last puddles. Valerie knew that she was expected in Miss Llivia's office when she was done mopping. Valerie wanted to throw up.

Completely exhausted, Valerie dragged herself and her wet soggy red gym shoes to Miss Llivia's office. Even the usually bright and cheery Miss Llivia looked mad. She was busy changing her wet shoes for the fresh dry brown slippers she kept in her office closet for special occasions such as this. As Miss Llivia changed, she told Valerie that tomorrow she would be working with Soha, head of the janitorial staff.

Then the phone rang, Miss Llivia spoke very seriously to the person on the other side of the phone. With her voice lowered, Miss Llivia swiveled her black leather chair around. Valerie was baffled as Miss Llivia continue to whisper mysteriously to her unknown caller. Valerie's curiosity peaked as she accidently dropped her yellow gloves next to miss Llivia's chair.

Miss Llivia rapidly turned her chair around and hung up the phone. Valerie was startled. Miss Llivia suddenly stood up and excused herself from the room. Valerie was confused. Valerie waited and waited. Valerie paced back and forth waiting for Miss Llivia to return. Nobody came, nobody left. Valerie continued to wait. Finally, Jaz came in, "Honey, Abigail is outside, waiting to take you home, please get your belongings and get to the bus before it's too late."

Valerie thought she finished another day in trouble, she was frustrated, why did bad things happen to good people. Abigail held the bus door open for Valerie and said, "Buenos Dias, Como Estas?" Valerie rudely did not answer. It had been months since Mt. Valerie had erupted, but today her attitude was being tested. Abigail did not know what happened but knew Mt. Valerie was building steam and there was nothing she could do or say to stop the explosion of attitude.

Mr. Dulany was outside fertilizing his lawn for the rough cold winter that was just a few months away. Abigail stopped the white hospital bus by Valerie's driveway and opened the bus door. Mt Valerie came off the bus with plenty of attitude. Abigail was scared, but Mt. Valerie did not scare Mr. Dulany, he had dealt with teenagers for years and with a little love and support Valerie would be fine.

As she flew up her driveway, she knew Mr. Dulany was going to give her some advice whether she wanted it or not. Not out of curiosity, but out of respect and politeness Valerie paused for his advice. Seizing the moment Mr. Dulany looked Valerie in the eyes and proclaimed, "Obstacles don't have to stop you. "If you run into a wall, do not turn around and give up, figure out how to climb it, go through it or work around it", a quote from Michael Jordan."

Valerie was not impressed, she huffed and puffed and shrugged her shoulders, Valerie rushed into her house, ran to her room and cried asking herself "Why? Why, did I listen to that bad, bad man Mr. Dulany?

Thursday

The Camouflaged Beast

Today was Thursday, Valerie woke up miserable. Two more days of this nightmare, two more days of training at Parkview hospital. Maybe she should quit, that would disappoint Mr. Dulany, maybe she should continue her quest, that would probably disappoint Miss Llivia. Valerie thought of William having the time of his life at McDonald's, he was probably the "Big Mac" by now, and Joseline working with the candy maker, what a sweet job, Valerie was jealous.

Last night her mother and father, ordered Panda Express, half fried rice and half chow Mein orange chicken, Valerie's favorite to cheer her up. This was a wonderful meal, a meal fit for the Gods, Valerie had two plates full, one plate too many, but thankfully this calmed Mt. Valerie down enough where the river of hot attitude never exploded. Valerie thought about how Mr. Dulany quoted Michael Jordan, "Obstacles don't have to stop you. If you run into a wall, do not turn around or give up, figure out how to climb it, go through it or go around it." Valerie fell asleep thinking about those wonderful words.

The next morning Valerie awoke in her comfy bed for moment thinking about those same words, her stomach was still digesting the two servings of orange chicken. Valerie's Mom yelled, "Valerie, Ya levantense, it is time to get up, the bus will be here in thirty minutes." Valerie started to get up and her stomach let out a rumble, but all Valerie could do was think about those words, figure out how to climb it, go through it or go around it. She repeated those words, climb it, go through it or go around it. "Valerie, do you hear me young lady? Ya levantense!" yelled her mother from the bottom of the long staircase.

Responding to her mother was not only respectful, but mandatory in Valerie's house. Valerie stood up quickly and her stomach growled, roared and turned upside down. Unfortunately, Valerie let out a very silent fart, silent but deadly. Vivian, her sister, covered herself in her blankets, fearing the world was coming to an end. Valerie thought she could compete with the boys any day.

Then it hit her, smashing into her brain like the water at Niagara Falls, or Jimmy doing a trey flip with his skateboard or her sister Vivian ferociously spiking the volleyball in one of her matches. "Of course, I got it!" exclaimed Valerie as she accidently farted again. Valerie jumped back into bed and covered herself with her warm mustard yellow blanket. Preparing her herself for the best theatrical performance ever.

"Mom, I don't feel good, my stomach hurts," Valerie painfully moaned. "Carumba, what is wrong?" her mother asked as she came up the stairs. Valerie quietly farted again. Her mother raced into their room only to be overcome with the large cloud of digested Panda Express coming from Valerie's tiny body. "Carumba! What died in here?" she asked. Valerie moaned again and rolled over.

Valerie's mother bravely tucked in her eldest daughter, kissed her and told Valerie, "Everything will be okay!" Her mother left the girl's room and went downstairs for a cup of coffee. At work Valerie's mom had a mandatory meeting about the progress of curing Covid-19. She got Vivian off to her school and finally poured that first elusive cup of coffee.

Valerie's Mom sat down and took a quick sip of the strong black coffee, then they heard the little bus, beep! Beep! Beep! Valerie's Mom realized she forgot to call the hospital. Quickly, she ran down the driveway to talk to the bus driver Abigail. Mr. Dulany was outside watering the fall mums, as she ran by him, she said "Buenos Dias!" Mr. Dulany was confused, where was Valerie. He watched as the little bus pulled away without Valerie, he was sad, Valerie found a way under the obstacle.

Worried, Mr. Dulany asked Valerie's Mom about Valerie. Valerie had to get up to use the bathroom, she saw the two adults talking as she passed by the window. Valerie's Mom explained everything, including missing the mandatory meeting, Mr. Dulany said he could help, his schedule was free all morning. Valerie came out of the bathroom feeling much better. She heard the front door close.

As Valerie headed back to her soft warm, smelly bed, she passed by the full length mirror the sisters shared. Yesterday, Valerie saw a young girl, with plenty of promise, good character and a future filled with hope. Valerie continued to stare at herself. Today, she saw a girl who was deceitful, a girl who lied, and a girl who manipulated her mother. She did not recognize this girl nor did she like the girl she saw in the mirror. Something had to change.

Fully dressed and ready to go to the hospital, Valerie came running down the stairs yelling "Mom! Mom! I am feeling much better, can you please take me to the hospital? Mr. Dulany came from the kitchen holding a cup of fresh brewed black coffee. Valerie was startled. "Where is my mom?" asked a concerned Valerie.

Mr. Dulany assured Valerie her mother was okay, "Your Mom had a mandatory meeting, your father is at work, you were sick and sleeping, my schedule was free, so I said I would be here just in case anything happened. Your mother will be back after her meeting."

Valerie bashfully replied, "I know I missed the bus, but I am feeling much better. Can you please take me to the hospital?" Mr. Dulany checked her temperature, 98.5, fine, texted to inform her mother and told Valerie, "Your chariot awaits you!" together they swiftly got in Mr. Dulany's 2017 Chevy Equinox. Valerie forgot how slow Mr. Dulany drove, but they did arrive safely.

He dropped Valerie off at the front of Parkview Hospital, he just smiled knowing Valerie had found a way over the obstacle. Mr. Dulany was proud of Valerie. She walked into the hospital, but there was no Miss Llivia. She went to the front desk where Jaz suggested that Valerie head to Miss Llivia's office.

Upon entering the office, Valerie noticed Miss Llivia talking to a young smaller girl with a huge smile. Miss Llivia noticed Valerie at the doorway of her office, "I thought your mother said you had a stomachache and were not able to come in today. I was just telling Soha, that you were not going to be here, but it looks like a change of plans. Soha meet Valerie, Valerie meet Soha." They shook each other's hand.

"Today you will be working with Soha, our Head Sanitation Officer." Valerie was confused, "I thought I was going to help the janitor today." Soha quickly answered, "Janitor is such a demeaning phrase, "Today as a junior sanitation officer, we will clean and scrub this hospital from top to bottom, we will pick up every piece of trash, empty every trash can and then take a well-deserved lunch break in the cafeteria. I hear the lunch special is a $2.99 chicken nugget special, my favorite"

Valerie was feeling kind of spunky, she asked Soha, "Doesn't a janitor clean, scrub, pick up trash and empty trash too?" Soha felt the attitude of the young teenage girl. "But we do it with style and grace, with dignity, with sophistication, with an air of nobility." Valerie continued the debate, "So we are Princess Picker-uppers?" Miss Llivia had enough, "Please go do your job Soha. Whether you are a Sanitation Officer, Janitor or a Princess Picker-upper."

"Excuse me Valerie, may I talk to you in private" politely asked Miss Llivia. Valerie was terrified, Miss Llivia was going to finally "talk" to her about all the bad things that had happened the last few days. The misguided visitors, the food fight, which was not her fault, the flooding, which was not her fault, Valerie hated being in trouble, or the center of attention. Miss Llivia made sure Soha was out of the room, then looked Valerie directly in the eyes.

"I have to warn you, Soha is known for being a little troublemaker." Valerie was confused, but Miss Llivia continued, "Soha likes to prank fellow employees and visitors with fake plastic bugs, snakes, anything she can get her hands on." Valerie did not believe her. "Here is the proof!" Miss Llivia stated as she opened the bottom drawer of her desk. Valerie saw plastic snakes, fake rats and hairy spiders. Miss Llivia slammed the desk drawer shut and told Valerie, "You have been warned, be careful!"

Outside the office, Soha was waiting patiently. Soha was wearing the latest bright blue jumpsuit, perfect for keeping her clothes clean, but she needed to get Valerie a jumpsuit too. Valerie decided a jumpsuit would not look on her, so she declined the fashion assistance, her blue jeans, red blouse and red gym shoes would be fine for today. Starting at the top floor, the seventh floor, Valerie cleaned, Valerie scrubbed, Valerie picked up trash and Valerie emptied the trash cans from each room into her cart.

Valerie ran into Mr. Hernandez from room 711 again, he had been pranked by Soha every day during his visit in Parkview Hospital. He seemed to be a nice guy but did not like the daily deliveries of artificial snakes he received. Mrs. Reynolds in room 738 did not like the big black rat that Soha left behind her bed last night. Mr. Mac despised the hairy scorpion, that Soha left on his breakfast tray. However, Izzy, the little girl who had a broken arm in room 744, loved the fake butterflies that Soha left on the window.

PART THREE

It was pretty-basic work, emptying the trash and keeping the rooms clean, but very important work. Soha never let up trying to scare Valerie, on the seventh floor Soha left a big red lobster on Valerie's cart, on the sixth floor, there was a big ugly beetle, on the fifth floor Soha left Valerie a big brown rattlesnake, Valerie was not amused or scared. After each floor, Valerie handed Soha back the creature and said, "I think you are losing your touch." However, Soha was not giving up.

On the fourth floor, Valerie found a tiny mouse on her cart. On the third floor after coming out of the girl's washroom there was a large plastic blue-eyed owl perched on her cleaning cart. Valerie was amused and impressed, but still not scared. Almost done with the second floor, Valerie was ready for an elephant, but there was nothing. Together Soha and Valerie cleaned the front lobby. There were no bugs, no snakes, no barn animals. Valerie wondered if Soha had given up.

Valerie said, "hi" to Jaz, as they cleaned the front lobby. Jaz noticed the cleaning carts. Almost everyone had threw the yogurt cups away that Elena had made for them. It looked good with strawberries, blueberries and raspberries, topped with walnuts. Jaz wondered why the nutritional treat was thrown away by so many of the patients. Jaz decided to save the yogurt cups for the furry friends in her backyard. The raccoons and squirrels would love this treat. Jaz went to get a box.

Soha and Valerie decided to head down to the cafeteria for lunch. The two had worked hard all morning cleaning the hospital. The $2.99 chicken nugget special would be the perfect meal to fill their tiny stomachs, but first they had to empty the cleaning carts into the big dumpster in the back of the hospital. Jaz came back with a box and was disappointed the girls were gone. Soha complimented Valerie on her cleaning skills as they opened the big navy-blue back door.

Shocked, Soha asked "Where is the dumpster?" Valerie did not know. Then Soha answered herself, "Today is Thursday, they replace and empty it every Thursday." Soha paused for a moment to think. "We can empty these after lunch, "I am hungry, how about you?" Valerie thought about leaving the garbage outside. "Won't the animals eat these?" asked Valerie. Soha wasn't concerned. Without thinking, Valerie who was having a stellar day and Soha who had been beaten by Valerie, left the overflowing carts outside and headed to the cafeteria for the $2.99 chicken nugget special.

Valerie and Soha were becoming friends, Valerie respected Soha's pranks and Soha respected Valerie for her hard work and positivity. Together they ate their chicken nuggets and French fries. Together they enjoyed Lipton's peach ice-tea. Valerie finally asked Soha, "So, why did you give up on pranking me?" Before going to the bathroom, Soha chuckled and eerily replied, "I haven't!" Valerie got goosebumps. Valerie was scared.

Soha was in the bathroom for a long time, Valerie was worried. Ashley saw Valerie and asked her if everything was okay. Ashley informed Valerie that Soha liked to disappear a lot, she was probably planning one of her hospital renowned pranks. Being impatient, a bad trait she learned from Mr. Dulany, Valerie decided to get back to being a Princess Picker-upper.

Having her stomach full and having a good morning gave Valerie a false sense of confidence. Valerie knew the cleaning carts had to be emptied before continuing be a sanitation officer. Valerie's mind wandered as she headed to the back of the big hospital, she thought about how rude she was to Mr. Dulany, how she ignored Mr. Dulany and how she disrespected their friendship. Valerie opened the big navy-blue back door and saw it, sitting on top of her cleaning cart.

Valerie was not scared. Valerie was not impressed. This "plastic" skunk did not even look real. Nonchalantly Valerie walked over to the "fake" white and black skunk and picked it up. The "fake" skunk did not move. Valerie thought she would be funny and bring the "fake" in the girl's bathroom where Soha was hiding. Visitors ran, patients ran, and employees ran as

Valerie walked down the hallway carrying the "fake" skunk. Soha was not hiding in the bathroom.

Unaware of what was happening, Valerie continued to carry the "fake" skunk looking for Soha. Next, Valerie headed to the cafeteria, where she had last seen Soha. Soha was sitting at the table, drinking the last of her ice-tea. Soha saw Valerie coming with the skunk and froze. Valerie showed the skunk to Soha and said, "Nice try!" Soha quietly saw the skunk squirm.

Valerie felt the skunk squirm also. Valerie nonchalantly told the skunk to settle down. Valerie immediately realized the "fake" skunk was real. Valerie screamed and dropped the scared skunk. Valerie froze and Soha ran out of the busy cafeteria. In an instant, the angry skunk positioned itself, raised it big furry black tail and sprayed Valerie from her red gym shoes to her freshly brushed black hair.

Miss Llivia did not want to see or smell Valerie in her office. Abigail refused to let Valerie on the bus. Valerie's mom was still at work. With big black plastic bags covering his seats and the windows wide open, Mr. Dulany picked Valerie up from the hospital. He had Valerie stand in her backyard while he retrieved some needed cleaning items.

Mr. Dulany came back carrying Dawn dish detergent, a bucket, a sponge and the hose. Valerie was confused, "I thought you used tomato juice when a skunk sprays you?" Valerie inquired. "Old wives' tale, Dawn actually breaks down the oils that the skunk secretes, that's why they use it on animals during oil spills" Mr. Dulany said. "Start scrubbing, this may take a while" Valerie was furious. Mt. Valerie was building steam.

Valerie scrubbed, and Mr. Dulany sprayed the hose. After two washings Mr. Dulany got Valerie a peanut butter and jelly sandwich and a couple of towels. It was fall and the warm afternoons soon turned to chilly evenings. Valerie did not say much during her De-skunking, she was too mad. Mr. Dulany gave Valerie some bit of unwanted advice, "It is during our darkest moment, that we must focus on the light"

Her mother pulled up, saw Valerie sopping wet as Mr. Dulany sprayed her with the garden hose. "Que' Paso"? What happened!" Mom cried as she ran to her daughter. Her mother thanked Mr. Dulany as she took over de-skunking Valerie. Mr. Dulany left without Valerie thanking him. After several more hours the humiliated Valerie was de-skunked, dried, and wrinkled. Valerie ran to her room crying "Why? Why, did I listen to that bad, bad man Mr. Dulany?"

Friday

The Cloaked Visitors

Today was Friday, the last day of her school supported field trip to Parkview Hospital. Today was the last day of this week-long nightmare. Today she must be volunteering, but Miss Llivia never told her officially what she would be doing on the last day. Valerie had left the hospital quickly yesterday, okay she was asked to leave because of the awful smell, but in her defense, she did not know the skunk was real. After embarrassingly being washed down outside for three hours, she was finally allowed to come inside and soak in the warm bathtub for two more hours in a lavender bath soap. Her mom decided to throw her clothes away, saying "They Stink! Ellos huelen!"

It was early, very early, the sun was not up yet, Valerie sniffed herself, no sign of skunk spray, thank goodness. Valerie felt like a raisin last night, her skin was shriveled from all the water, but she was dried out today and back to normal, thank goodness. Valerie thought about Mr. Dulany's advice every morning and evening, she wouldn't have to listen to it anymore, thank goodness. Valerie laid in bed looking out the window, it was dark, pitch dark. Valerie wondered how Sophia, the gamer was doing, probably having the best week of her life beating the pro gamer, George Thompson, and she thought about Amiya who was spending a week, learning to be a better comic, Valerie was jealous.

As she laid in her comfortable warm bed, she thought about the report she would have to write for Monday morning. Valerie continued to stare out the window when she saw a small white light alternating with a red light, this small light made Valerie think about what Mr. Dulany had said yesterday, "In our darkest moment, we must focus on the light." Valerie laughed. The flashing lights bothered her, so she turned over and started thinking about the report again.

Valerie thought to herself, "What am I going to write in my report? I learned how to send people to the wrong room, I learned how to cause a food fight, I learned how to flood a hospital and I learned how to be sprayed by a skunk?" Valerie laughed at herself as she fell back asleep, not realizing those flashing red and white lights were there for her sweet neighbor and friend, Mr. Dulany.

Morning came and Valerie felt better about going back to the hospital to finish the week, she was glad she didn't quit, she was glad she had this experience, and she was glad she listened to her good friend and neighbor Mr. Dulany. As she finished her small glass of fresh squeezed orange juice, Abigail beeped the horn to the little white bus, beep! Beep! Beep!

Happy as a lark, Valerie unexpectantly said, "Te Quiero!" and kissed her mother goodbye. Her mother was confused and wondered what had gotten into Valerie. Her sweet annoying sister was also in the kitchen eating breakfast, she was still half asleep eating her Apple Jacks when Valerie walked over and hugged Vivian, also telling her "Yo tambien te quiero!" Vivian was also confused and wondered what had gotten into Valerie. Almost as if she had read their minds Valerie said, "I have seen the light," and walked out the front door.

Abigail was waiting patiently for Valerie in the bus, but Valerie realized something was wrong. The mysterious feeling gave Valerie goosebumps. Before getting on the little white hospital bus Valerie looked to the right, nothing, she looked to the left nothing, and she looked behind her, nothing, but something was wrong, something was missing.

Mr. Dulany was picked up by the Glenside paramedics at 6:03 a.m. As usual he woke up early and had his black coffee, thought he took his carbidopa-levodopa, walked his disappearing garden, and checked his laptop computer for any important emails. When he walked, he noticed his left foot was swollen and his leg was in pain, he went inside and took two ibuprofen tablets, hoping the swelling would decline. After an unusually long hour, the pain persisted, and the swelling increased.

Unfortunately, Mr. Dulany had to get help, the pain was unbearable had this point. Unfortunately, he had to wake up his wife, she liked to stay up late and sleep in, quite the opposite of Mr. Dulany. Unfortunately, Mr. Dulany was downstairs, and Mrs. Dulany was upstairs. Fortunately, Mrs. Dulany was concerned and alarmed at the dangerous swelling. Fortunately, she immediately called 911.

Valerie was dropped off in the front of Parkview Hospital, just like all the other days. Valerie was sad, it was an unusual week, but she enjoyed being here, and it was coming to an end. She learned a lot about being a receptionist, she learned so much in the cafeteria and working with the landscapers. Soha had a tough job, but she made it fun and enjoyable.

Miss Llivia was at the front desk waiting for Valerie. Inconspicuously, Miss Llivia took a whiff of Valerie, to make sure the young lady did not smell like a skunk. Valerie noticed Miss Llivia smelling her but was in no position to call her out on her rudeness. However, Valerie was thankful her mother rubbed a lavender Bounce fabric sheet all over her to remove any stubborn skunk residue. Thank goodness Mr. Dulany knew how to remove the smell the right way. She thought "I should listen to him more often," and that is when it hit her. "Where was Mr. Dulany this morning? he was always outside making sure his favorite neighbor made it to school" she asked herself.

Another very pretty-young lady walked up to Valerie, Miss Llivia introduced Valerie to Isabella and Isabella to Valerie. Valerie was stunned at Isabella's beauty. "Are we modeling today?" asked Valerie. Miss Llivia quickly corrected Valerie, "Isabella is our head candy striper, you will be working with her today." Excited Valerie asked, "Will we be making candy canes?"

Isabella chuckled at Valerie, "A candy striper is a term used for hospital volunteers. It was developed years ago as a term for high school students who took a mandatory community service class in order to graduate. The name stuck and anybody can be a candy striper today, boy, girl, man, woman, young or old." Valerie was intrigued. "But what does a candy striper do?" asked Valerie.

"We are the finishing touches on a hospital stay, we put the candles on a birthday cake. The doctors take care of the illness, the nurses help the doctors get the patient well, the receptionist welcomes everybody to the hospital, the dietician makes sure everybody eats right, the landscaper makes sure this hospital looks good on the outside and the janitors and housekeepers keep the hospital clean on the inside. We my dear, put the ketchup on the fries, we put the ice cubes in ice-tea, we have the ranch dressing for the carrot sticks. We make sure each patient gets their mail, gifts, balloons and flowers that loved ones send. If possible, we get anything the patient needs while they are in Parkview Hospital" Isabella proudly stated.

Valerie was intrigued, "so, we go around putting ketchup on people's fries and birthday candles on cakes?" Miss Llivia laughed and made sure Valerie was going to be okay, Isabella told Miss Llivia everything was under control, she would personally watch Valerie today. Isabella was an excellent candy striper, but tough. Miss Llivia was relieved. Isabella took

Valerie to the gift shop where she was introduced to her fellow candy stripers Jeannette and Andrea'.

Mr. Dulany was still at the hospital he was taken from the emergency room to room 138. His leg was still swollen, and the doctors could not figure out why. The doctors probed and prodded him, the nurses gave him pain killers, ibuprofen and an endless supply of ice packs. Mr. Dulany kept his leg up, and often took short naps while he waited for a diagnosis. His blood pressure was taken,134/78, his temperature was taken, 98.6, and the nurses regularly came and checked on his leg. The doctors were baffled.

Word soon spread throughout the Glendale Heights community that Mr. Dulany was in the hospital. Teachers from Hallsberry School sent cards wishing Mr. Dulany a quick recovery. Children from Hallsberry School sent cards and flowers. His relatives sent helium balloons. As usual, all gifts were sent to the hospital gift shop to be given to the candy stripers to pass out and to cheer up the patients.

Isabella was a very talented candy-striper. Not only did she have a heart of gold, she was incredibly tough, but had a smile that would melt a steel candy bar on a cold day. There was no official uniform, except a smile, but Isabella had a formula for being the best candy striper in the Parkview hospital. Her mission was simple, teach everyone she worked with how to work hard and fast like her.

Andrea' and Jeannette had volunteered with Isabella for many months now, they were very good, but Isabella felt they needed to pick up their speed. Isabella called a quick huddle before letting the girls cheer up the patients. Very calmly she called them over, "Andrea', Jeannette, Valerie! Come on over, we need to prep before we go out." Jeannette came quickly over as well as Andrea', Valerie was astonished with the number of cards, balloons and gifts that were in the gift shop and questioned how they were going to deliver so many gifts in a day.

Isabella was quick with an answer, "First there are four of us, Second I have some time-tested rules that we use to get you in and out of a patient's room politely and gracefully. Third, most of them are for a man in room 138." Jeannette, Andrea' and Valerie looked at the humungous stack of gifts, and simultaneously said "Really?" "Don't worry girls, we will be done in time to enjoy the $2.99 fish and chip lunch special in the cafeteria."

I learned a phrase many years ago when I went to Hallsberry School, a very wise man once told me "Smile and the whole world smiles with you" Valerie had heard that somewhere before, it sounded very familiar, she asked "Who was that wiseman?" Isabella thought for a moment and said "Mr. Dulany." Valerie wondered again where Mr. Dulany was this morning.

"We start on the seventh floor, we knock on the door say good morning, talk about the weather, small talk, stay away from their name and why they are in the hospital. Keep the conversation light and positive. If the patient is not there or asleep just leave them on the table." The girls were excited, Andrea' smiled, Jeannette smiled, and Valerie was confused. Seeing the look of confusion on Valerie's face, Isabella leaned over and whispered into Valerie's ear "Don't worry Valerie, just stick with me and we will be fine." Valerie let out a big sigh of relief.

Jeannette, Andrea', Valerie and Isabella rode the rickety elevator to the seventh floor. The cart carrying the balloons, cards, stuffed animals and gifts was overloaded, the girls were small, but so was the elevator. It was almost like a can of sardines, but with no smelly fish. Jeannette and Andrea' took this ride before, they were excited. Valerie was nervous. Isabella took charge and told her troops to get ready for battle.

Isabella took the lead getting out of the elevator. Jeannette followed fixing her pretty floral dress and wearing her best smile. Andrea came next brushing her beautiful raven hair and wearing her best smile. Having some incredible complex days filled with bad luck, Valerie was apprehensive about getting off the elevator, Isabella took her hand and helped her off the elevator. Jeannette and Andrea' retrieved the cart.

Andrea' grabbed the two stuffed animals, a teddy bear and a penguin with a "Get Well" balloon and a large handful of get-well cards from her classmates in Mrs. Marino class for the adorable girl with the broken arm in room 744, Izzy. Jeannette grabbed the sunflowers and the cards for the sweet older lady in room 738, Mrs. Reynolds. Isabella took the three cards for a young lady named Samantha, who cut her finger last week trying to make fresh pasta. Ill-fated, she waited a week before taking care of her laceration on her index finger, somehow, somewhere it became infected. Valerie was left with a balloon for Mr. Hernandez in room 711.

The balloon read "Your #1" Valerie took it and headed to room 711. Valerie entered quietly. Mr. Hernandez was busy working on his laptop, he was concentrating on his work and Valerie wanted to be invisible. Mr. Hernandez saw Valerie tying the balloon to the table and mentioned "You're not helping Soha plant snakes in my room, are you?" Startled, Valerie was speechless. Mr. Hernandez was a man of many words, "I have seen you as the receptionist, in the cafeteria, planting outside, cleaning inside and now inside doing who knows what this week. What are you doing?

"I am training to be a nurse." Valerie replied. Mr. Hernandez was impressed with Valerie and wanted to know more. Valerie sat down and began talking to Mr. Hernandez. Besides Mr. Dulany, very rarely did anyone want to hear anything Valerie wanted to share. Mr. Hernandez put down his computer and began listening to Valerie. Turns out Mr. Hernandez was a nice guy. Together the two talked, and talked, and talked.

Isabella finished with Samantha and returned to deliver balloons to another man in room 701, Mr. Gomez. Andrea' finished with Izzy in record time and came back to get the lilies for Ms. Brown in room 713. Jeannette talked with Mrs. Reynolds for a bit and worked her way back to the gift cart for some flowers for someone named Carisa in room 789, she was all the way down the hallway because she liked to play her music loud. Valerie was still in room 711 talking to Mr. Hernandez.

Jeannette waited patiently. Andrea' waited patiently. Isabella knew the rule, she made the rule, go in, say hi, leave the gift, wish them well and leave. Valerie was talking, talking too much, Valerie was breaking the rules. Isabella politely told Mr. Hernandez that Valerie had other patients to visit, and she needed to go. Isabella gently took Valerie's hand and left room 711. Mr. Hernandez was filled with sorrow.

The clock moved quickly on this cool fall morning. Together Jeannette and Andrea' moved swiftly finishing the sixth floor in record time. Isabella went nowhere without Valerie, together they swiftly liberated the balloons and flowers from the cart, wished the patients well and quickly left the room. Valerie did not get to know anybody's name or why they were in the hospital.

The four quickly made minced meat out of the fifth, fourth and third floors. Valerie's legs were tired. Valerie's kidneys were about to explode. Valerie's mouth was parched. Unexpectantly, Valerie saw a wooden bench on the second floor and requested "Can we take a break?" Without waiting for permission, Valerie plopped her tiny body down on the wooden bench. Jeannette was mystified, Andrea' was shocked and Isabella was fuming.

Almost out of breath, Valerie told Isabella, Jeannette and Andrea', "To pop a squat". Exhausted herself, Jeannette sat down. Isabella frowned. Seeing Jeannette bravely sit down, the fatigued Andrea' wisely also chose to pop a squat, Isabella continued to frown. Valerie quickly ran to the bathroom as Jeannette and Andrea' sat on the bench. Isabella started to fume. Jeannette and Andrea' quickly followed Valerie to the bathroom. Isabella stood there just staring at the doorway to the bathroom.

Smiling, laughing and chit chatting, the three young creatures emerged from the girl's bathroom, extremely ecstatic about their empty kidneys. As the three bonded around the water fountain the powerful

Isabella began circling the three thirsty but innocent young ladies just waiting to pounce on her victim. Valerie sensed something was wrong, suddenly she got goosebumps.

Valerie let Jeannette drink from the water first, like a thirsty gazelle who was migrating across the great plains of Africa, Jeannette drank like a fish. Next was Andrea' who also drank forever, coming up only once for fresh air. Valerie rubbed her goosebumps wondering what she was missing. Isabella continued to patiently wait for her victim. Jeannette saw Isabella waiting and wisely stood by the cart, perfectly still, perfectly quiet. After finishing her long drink of water, Andrea' saw Isabella waiting to pounce and wisely went over to the gift cart and stood by Jeannette, perfectly still, perfectly quiet.

Was Valerie a camel? Where was she storing all this water? Valerie continued to drink the nectar, totally unfocused on what was happening around her. Isabella was coming in for the attack, Jeannette could not look, Andrea' felt ashamed, both were stuck in a trans. Valerie finished the drink and slowly turned around ready to get back to being a candy-striper. Relentless in her ambition, the powerful Isabella went in for the kill.

Mr. Dulany was still in room 138 waiting for the authorization to go home. The swelling in his left leg had subsided and he was feeling much better, the excoriating pain was gone. After a battery of tests and a lengthy conversation with the neurologist, it was determined Mr. Dulany had forgotten to take his Parkinson's medicine, the carbidopa-levodopa. He was ordered bed rest for a week and told he could go home.

Valerie swallowed the remaining water, stood back up and wiped her dripping wet mouth. "That's just what I needed! Time to finish the second floor." Pouncing furiously Isabella quickly approached Valerie. "Need a drink of water?" graciously asked Valerie. Angrily Isabella replied, "No, I need a word with you!" Valerie was mystified.

Isabella took Valerie over to the corner. "I am not happy, young lady. First, you took way too long in Mr. Hernandez's room. You broke our rule of in and out quickly, strike 1. Second, you took an unauthorized break, strike 2." "But......" explained Valerie. Valerie was quickly cutoff by Isabella, "There will be no buts. One more strike and I will have to ask you to leave." Valerie was crushed, Andrea' said, "She said there will be no buts." Jeannette and Andrea laughed.

In a very demanding voice, Isabella commanded the three young ladies to finish the second-floor gifts. Mr. Webster in room 223 had been sent a dictionary for a gift, Mrs. Hallmark had a stack of get-well cards that needed to be delivered to 210 and The Helium's in room 261, who just had a baby boy named Gaston, had several bouquets of balloons that needed to be delivered. Isabella reminded the candy stripers about their time spent in the room, go in, say hi, leave the gift and say goodbye.

Jeannette took the dictionary to Mr. Webster, Andrea took the get-well cards to Mrs. Hallmark, and Isabella watched Valerie very carefully while she delivered the balloons to the proud new parents, the Helium's. Isabella was very excited, however because of Valerie they were one floor behind, but it was lunchtime. The first floor would have to wait until after lunch.

"Lunch!" exclaimed Isabella. Jeannette quickly started pushing the card to the elevator, Andrea quickly followed with Valerie and Isabella determined to catch up. Valerie was famished. Isabella hit the elevator button and the cold metal elevator door quickly sprung open. Standing patiently in the small elevator was Mr. Hernandez, Isabella cordially said, "Hi", however Mr. Hernandez did not reply. On the first floor he quickly exited, not saying a word.

Not concerned about Mr. Hernandez, Jeannette, Andrea', Isabella and Valerie all rode the small elevator down to the lower level to the increasingly popular hospital cafeteria for the $2.99 fish and chips special.

Isabella quickly declared she was buying, Jeannette got excited, Andrea' was thankful but Valerie was intrigued. Valerie quickly took out her pocket-sized candy-striper rule book. Valerie opened the rule book to page 4, paragraph 6, line 27. She showed it to Isabella, "In appreciation of their efforts, any candy striper who volunteers a full day is entitled to a free lunch compliments of the hospital office." Isabella read the small manual and did not say a word.

The three ate their fish and chips quickly. Jeannette splattered ketchup all over her plate, making it look like a crime scene. Andrea' dipped her fried fish and French fries in the ranch sauce meant for the celery sticks. Valerie loved fish, cod, oysters, and crabs but was not too sure of this fish, she passed on the fries. Isabella sulked when she took her fish, knowing that Valerie had beaten her. All four had the ice-tea. At the end of the 30 minutes Isabella commanded everyone back to work, they still had the first floor to pass out the cards, gifts, flowers and balloons.

Mr. Dulany was home now, Mrs. Dulany had waited all morning with him and brought him home. Now the trick was to keep him off his feet, he loved keeping busy and always kept himself occupied. When watching television, he usually got up during commercials trying to accomplish something. When he turned on the coffee pot in the morning, he usually cleaned the kitchen, not wanting to waste time. Even when he took a shower, he wiped down the walls and shelves trying to keep the downstairs bathroom clean. Mr. Dulany did not know how to relax; relaxation was not in his vocabulary.

Coming home Mr. Dulany was disappointed he did not see Valerie. Parkview was a small community hospital, and he wanted to congratulate her on finishing the week. Mr. Dulany wanted to leave a message in the room, a message only Valerie would know he left. Although it was very hard to write, Mr. Dulany scribbled out a small message, "People will forget what you said, people will forget what you did, but people will never forget how you made them feel." Before leaving room 138, he folded the piece of paper and left it on the uncomfortable sanitized white pillow.

Andrea' retrieved the cart from the hallway while Jeannette used the bathroom. Isabella picked up her trash and threw it in the over-flowing brown trash can. Valerie went by Andrea' waiting for further instructions. Isabella upset that the first floor was not finished yet, told the girls, "After we finish the first floor, we need to help Stephanie in the gift shop. Every Friday we need to take inventory. Valerie, please stay with me at all times, so we can finish delivering the gifts." Begrudgingly, Valerie shook her head yes just hoping to finish the week with no more drama.

As the tiny elevator climbed from the lower level to the first floor Valerie began to think about her other classmates on their school sponsored career weeks. Amari was probably being hoisted up on his team's shoulders for throwing the perfect spiral pass in a crucial last-minute touchdown winning the game for his team. Camilla was gloating over her picture-perfect photo cover for Vogue magazine and discussing her world tour her and Kylie Jenner would go on. Joseline probably developed a new candy bar, and it was going to be named after her. The Joseline Bar, filled with crunchy peanuts, creamy caramel and only the finest chocolate. Isabella suddenly asked, "Valerie are you coming?"

Valerie grabbed the cart, it was still very full of flowers, cards and balloons, mostly for room 138, Valerie got goosebumps. Isabella started to pass out the gifts for the patients, Jeannette why don't you take everything for room 112, Andrea' take the balloons for room 176 and Valerie, you and I will take the cards for room 144. Remember girls, say hello, drop the gift, wish them well and leave." Scared, the three girls shook their heads in agreement. Quickly and efficiently Jeannette and Andrea' returned, Valerie barely saw the person in room 144, but Isabella was proud of her fellow candy stripers for making quick work of their assignments.

Isabella realized there was only three rooms left. Proudly, Isabella told Andrea to take the flowers and cards to room 173 and Jeannette to take the cards and balloons to room 114. Isabella told Valerie they would start unloading all the gifts for room 138. Eerily, Valerie got the goosebumps again. Andrea' and Jeannette quickly left. Isabella's phone rang, Isabella looked at the caller id and quickly answered the phone. Valerie quietly asked what she was to do, but Isabella put her finger in the air indicating she should wait.

Valerie waited and waited, but like Mr. Dulany, she was a little impatient. Isabella was distracted with an awkward look on her face, Valerie wondered if her goldfish had died, or maybe somebody found her broom, broken and abandoned on the side of the road. Valerie figured there was no reason she couldn't start bringing the gifts into room 138 while Isabella was on the phone. With Isabella focused on the phone call, Valerie grabbed two sunflower plants and brought them to room 138. The goosebumps appeared again causing Valerie to shiver.

Having not seen the message on the pillow, Valerie went back to get some more sunflowers, Mr. Dulany's favorite. She carefully brought them into room 138 and put them on the windowsill, still not noticing the message on the pillow. Jeannette was done with room 112 so she decided to help bring in the first box of get-well cards for room 138, Jeannette put them on the small nightstand next to the bed, Jeannette did not notice the message on the pillow. Andrea finished delivering the assorted birthday balloons for room 176, Andrea quickly said Happy Birthday and tried to leave. Mrs. Lopez, who had a broken hand and spoke broken English, asked Andrea' "NO se ingles, me duele la mano puedes, mandar una enferma? (My hand really hurts can you send me a nurse?)"

Andrea' respected Isabella's rules., however this was a time to break the rules, this was a time to do the right thing, Mrs. Lopez needed her help. Trying to avoid Isabella's wrath, Andrea ran swiftly to find a nurse for the lady. At the end of the hallway coming from room 157, Andrea' approached the pretty lady and read her name tag, it read "Nurse Deisy" "Can you please help Mrs. Lopez in room 176? She says she has a lot of pain and does not speak English." Without a hesitation, Nurse Deisy ran to room 176 to help Mrs. Lopez. Andrea' went to help Valerie and Jeannette with room 138.

Isabella was still on the phone whisper arguing with someone. With no one in the room to talk to there was no reason for Isabella to get mad at Valerie so Valerie continued to take some more marigolds to room 138 still not noticing the message but still getting goosebumps. Andrea' brought in the last handful of homemade cards from his friends at Hallsberry School, putting the unique cards on the small nightstand with the other cards. Andrea' still did not see the message left on the pillow.

Jeannette cleaned off the cart by removing the rest of the balloons. There was a Your#1 balloon, one get-well balloon with daisies on it and a get-well balloon with a cemetery marker on it, cruel, but funny. Jeannette tied the balloons on the bed railing, Jeannette still did not see the message on the pillow. Finally, they were done and decided to tidy up the room. Andrea' straightened the bathroom towels, Jeannette swept the floor and Valerie decided to make the bed. Valerie found the elusive message, opened it and deciphered the terrible handwriting, "People will forget about what you said, people will forget about what you did, but people will never forget how you made them feel!" Valerie got goosebumps.

Valerie just stared at the message, she recognized the thought and the handwriting. In her mind she said to herself, "Mr. Dulany was here, that's why he wasn't at his driveway this morning. He was here!" Valerie just stared at the message. Isabella got off the phone with Miss Llivia and ordered everyone out to the cart. Jeannette scurried out of the room. Andrea' left without a peep, but Valerie went over to read whose name was on the cards, it was Mr. Dulany's.

"People will forget what you say, people will forget what you did, but people will never forget how you made them feel!" Valerie said aloud, "He was here, sick and hurt and I didn't know!" Isabella was still upset about the call from Miss Llivia, and she took it out on Valerie's insubordination. "Valerie, Let's GO!" Isabella yelled. Valerie was still immersed in her thought about Mr. Dulany being in the hospital, she ignored Isabella.

"Valerie! Let's Go! We have to take inventory in the gift shop!" Isabella bellowed. Valerie didn't hear Isabella. Valerie started to read the message again but was quickly grabbed by Isabella. "Miss Llivia wants to see me after work, something about what you said" Isabella told Valerie. Defending herself, Valerie exclaimed, "I said nothing!" Isabella was mad and tried pulling Valerie out of room 138, Valerie refused to leave.

Completely losing her cool, Isabella went into a wild frenzy of raw uncontrolled emotion. "I ask for simple things for you and you refuse to listen. Another teenage know it all, that's all you are. I gave you two warnings, two strikes this morning for your insubordination, now I have no other choice, but you have just forced me to give you another for refusing to listen. Strike three, you are out of here, fired, do you understand?"

Valerie was mystified. How could she be fired from a volunteer job? Valerie was shocked "Where was Mr. Dulany?" Valerie was worried. Was Mr. Dulany, okay? Isabella was fuming! Valerie stood there wondering what to do. Mt. Isabella was ready to explode, impatient and tired of Valerie she loudly exploded "Get out and stay out!"

Terrified and upset Valerie ran out of the room 138 crying hysterically. Valerie wondered who encouraged her to stay the entire week. Valerie wondered who put her through this terrible week. She ran past Jaz at the receptionist desk, she ran through the front doors of the hospital, past Abigail's bus and down the street crying all the way to her house on Terry Road. She ran crying through the front door and to her bedroom yelling "Why? Why did I listen to that bad, bad man Mr. Dulany?"

The Weekend

The Inconspicuous Visitor

Valerie spent the entire Friday evening hidden in her room. This was her first job, and she was fired, her whole life she had wanted to become a nurse and in one disastrous week filled with embarrassment, accidents and frustrating events, her dreams of becoming a nurse were evaporating faster than a water spill on a 100-degree day in July. Maybe she should become a firefighter, maybe a policeman, maybe a rocket scientist. Then she thought she would probably send the astronaut to Pluto, so she quickly decided against it. Wallowing in self-pity, Valerie decided it was best she stayed in her room for the night.

Her sister Vivian was having a sleepover with her best-friend Sherlyn, so she was not in danger of hurting her. Her parents tried talking to her, but Valerie did not want to talk. Her Mom made a delicious seafood dinner with crab, oysters, mussels and lobster, but Valerie did not want to eat. Her Dad was watching their favorite television show, Guys Grocery Games, but Valerie did not want to watch. Valerie wanted to stay in her room and be alone.

Once again, she read the message left on the pillow, "people will forget what you said, people will forget what you did, but people will never forget how you made them feel." Valerie sighed and fell backwards on the bed.

"What have I done? Mr. Dulany will forget me! I made Mr. Dulany feel terrible." Disgusted in herself, what kind of friend was she? She answered herself, "A terrible one!" With tears in her eyes, she eventually fell asleep.

Saturday morning came, thank goodness. There was no hospital lesson today, thank goodness. Valerie wondered if she could stay in bed all day and avoid the world. Then Valerie thought about the day, she had chores to do, empty the dishwasher and vacuum the floors, not the end of the world. She needed to do her report on her work experience at the hospital, difficult, but Valerie had a talent for writing, not the end of the world. Valerie thought about the last job she HAD to do, visit Mr. Dulany, embarrassing and it could be the end of the world.

Nonchalantly and trying to be invisible Valerie slithered her way downstairs to do her chores. Valerie tried to be invisible, but the dishes did not cooperate. The plates and bowls banged together as she pulled them from the dishwasher, the silverware made a thunderous noise against each other as Valerie put them in the drawer and the glasses pinged each other as they were put in the brown cabinet above the dishwasher. Mom and Dad never got up to see Valerie.

One down one to go. Next Valerie needed to vacuum, the kitchen and living room where Mom and Dad were watching television. Dad was on his computer reading the news and Mom was on her laptop figuring out assorted crossword puzzles, they really were not watching the home improvement show, Good Bones. Valerie turned on the Dyson upright vacuum causing Mom and Dad to stare at Valerie. No words were said as Valerie rolled the vacuum over the carpet, under the couch, under the chairs and under the tables. Valerie worked her way through the living room, and into the kitchen. She turned off the vacuum and rolled up the eight-foot brown cord and pushed the vacuum into the hallway linen closet.

Thankful no one was talking, Valerie carefully worked her way back to the staircase, hoping to escape to her room, where no one bothered her, where she was a powerful princess, where she could wallow in her self-pity. Just as Valerie grabbed the stairwell, her mom said, "There's a fresh butter pecan coffee cake on the counter and I just filled the carafe with hot black coffee."

Powerful words, Mom was clever. Most people would be confused with fresh butter pecan coffee cake and hot black coffee, but Valerie knew what Mom was saying, those were Mr. Dulany's favorite. Valerie quietly replied "Okay," and took a step up. Mom did not say a word. Valerie took a second step up and stopped. Dad continued to read the news. Valerie took another step. Mom continued to work on her crossword puzzle, only breaking the awkward silence by asking Dad, "Do you know a five-letter word for feeling bad?"

Dad thought about it for a minute, "Sadly, I really don't know!" Valerie suddenly yelled "guilt" and ran quickly up the stairs, slamming the door. Mom looked lovingly at Dad and said, "I thought we had her!" Dad stared at Mom with a hunger in his eyes. "Now can I open up the coffee cake?" Mom thought about it and sadly replied, "Yes".

Dad slowly got up out of his big black recliner, stretched and slowly approached the kitchen. Then Dad felt the ground shake, the flower vase shook, and Dad braced himself. The staircase rumbled as Valerie came stampeding down. With her face washed, her brownish hair brushed and wearing her designer Levi jeans with a sapphire blue sweatshirt, Valerie swooped up the coffee cake and the carafe of hot black coffee and ran out the back door. Dad was heartbroken. Mom was ecstatic.

Valerie's Mom smiled, as she let the back-door slam shut. Valerie walked slowly toward Mr. Dulany's house. Up the concrete driveway, up the three stairs. Knock! Knock! Knock! Thinking no-one was home Valerie turned around and slowly started walking away. "Good morning, Valerie!"

exclaimed a very excited Mrs. Dulany. "How are you doing?" Mrs. Dulany continued as Valerie stood there with a blank look on her face.

Mrs. Dulany noticed the carafe and the coffee cake and realized why Valerie was there. "Please come in, let me take those from you." Valerie handed the carafe and the coffee cake to Mrs. Dulany, "Is Mr. Dulany home?" Mrs. Dulany smiled, "He has been expecting you, why don't you sit down, and I will get him." Valerie sat down on the big blue couch and waited. Only Bella the cat visited Valerie.

After what seemed liked hours, but was less than five minutes, Mr. Dulany came down the short staircase and saw Valerie, he smiled and stared. Valerie saw Mr. Dulany and smiled. He finally got himself to the bottom of the staircase, still smiling he opened his arms, Valerie came running. They hugged each other for an eternity. With a tear in her eye Valerie told Mr. Dulany she was "Sorry". With a tear in his eye Mr. Dulany said, "No Worries!"

They eventually sat down on the couch, with Mr. Dulany putting his leg up. Mrs. Dulany poured Mr. Dulany a cup of the hot black coffee and sliced the butter pecan coffee cake. She brought Valerie a nice cold glass of Minute Maid pulp free orange juice. "I think I will let you two talk, call me if you need anything!"

Mr. Dulany sipped his coffee and was quiet. Valerie sipped her orange juice and was quiet. The awkward silence filled the quiet living room. "I can water for you later, if you need me to" bashfully stated Valerie. "That would be nice" replied Mr. Dulany. The awkward silence returned to the room. Both Valerie and Mr. Dulany grabbed a piece of the fresh coffee cake.

Valerie suddenly burst out "Are you mad at me?" Mr. Dulany finished chewing his coffee cake and washed it down with a big gulp of the hot black coffee, "How could I ever be mad at you?" he quietly asked. Valerie sheepishly replied, "You were sick, in the hospital, where I was working, and I didn't even know it!" "But did you find the message I left on the pillow?" asked Mr. Dulany.

Valerie pulled the message from her pocket, they both laughed. They talked about the terrible week at the hospital and laughed hysterically at everything that had happened to Valerie. After several hours of small talk with Mr. Dulany, she finally mustered enough courage to ask for help with her paper due on Monday. "What do I write?" asked a confused Valerie.

"How am I going to make this look good, it was a complete nightmare. I misdirected people, I caused a food fight, I flooded the hospital, I brought a skunk into the hospital, and I got fired from a volunteer position. I will be the laughingstock of the middle school." Mr. Dulany listened intently.

"They will call it Valerie's Law, what can go wrong will go wrong. William probably had a great week at McDonald's, Joseline probably made delicious candy bars, Sophia probably beat the professional video gamer, Amari is probably the newest quarterback for the Bears, Camilla is the newest cover girl for Vogue and Amiya will be telling jokes at the comedy club. I will never be a nurse." Mr. Dulany listened intently.

Valerie continued talking about her paper describing her week at Parkview Hospital. "I know I will put a positive spin on it, whitewash it. I will tell them how I flawlessly escorted visitors throughout the hospital, I will write how I single handily kept the cafeteria clean during a very busy lunch rush, I will describe how I planted beautiful flowers and how I tried to educate people on wildlife. I won't bring up the whole getting fired from the volunteer position, otherwise I really will be the laughingstock at the middle school." Mr. Dulany listened intently.

Mr. Dulany snagged the last piece of the butter pecan coffee cake, suddenly the doorbell rang. Valerie offered to see who was there. It was Valerie's Mom, "Time to come home sweetheart." Valerie was disappointed but told her mom she would be home very soon. Not wanting to waste the moment, he very quietly said, "about your paper, speak with honesty, think with sincerity and act with integrity." Valerie's Mom was waiting outside, "Are you coming sweetheart?" Valerie gave Mr. Dulany a huge hug and left.

Mom needed to run to Target and liked when Valerie went with her. Together at Target, they purchased a gallon of 2% milk, two jalapeno peppers, a 12-count package of Mission corn tortillas and a two-pound brick of hot pepper cheese. Valerie tried feverishly to get her mother to get a snack at the Panda Express across from the Target, but her mother refused to cooperate. Valerie brought in the groceries for her mother and was told to work on her paper until dinner was ready.

Valerie went upstairs and sat down at the desk. Her sister, Vivian, was on her bed wearing her headphones reading the fifth Harry Potter book, "Harry Potter and the Order of the Phoenix". Valerie started thinking about what Mr. Dulany said, "Speak with honesty, think with sincerity and act with integrity." Valerie started typing on the laptop computer. Vivian saw Valerie typing and was curious.

Vivian took off her headphones and slowly snuck behind Valerie, she started reading what Valerie was writing, "it was a rough week, I caused mass confusion, a food fight." Vivian started laughing surprising Valerie, "What are you doing?" asked a mystified Vivian, "You have to sugar coat it." Abruptly, the doorbell rang. Vivian yelled, "I got it, it's probably Ashley and Brianna coming over to borrow my soccer ball!" Vivian ran downstairs to greet her two best friends.

Ashley, Brianna and Valerie sprinted back upstairs to get the soccer ball. Valerie was still on the computer typing. Vivian confidently read Valerie's sad report out loud to her friends, "I caused mass confusion, a food fight, flooding and a gas leak at the hospital this week." Ashley and Brianna laughed. Valerie was embarrassed. Vivian told Valerie she needed to spice the report up.

Vivian was a straight A student, she worked hard, played hard and studied hard. Valerie was intrigued. Vivian said, "If you don't change this report, you will be the laughingstock of the middle school!" "What about honesty?" Valerie asked. Brianna stepped in "You want the school to know you caused mass flooding and you caused a food fight? I don't think so, improvise and say you stopped the flooding, and you stopped the food fight!" "What about sincerity?" asked Valerie.

Ashley agreed with Vivian and Brianna. "Make it into a positive experience, you know the glass being half full instead of half empty. In your report blame the confusion on the receptionist and say you were the hero and helped with the confusion, with the skunk, blame it on the janitor, saying she was terrible at her job, and you were the hero by grabbing the skunk." "What about integrity?" asked Valerie.

The three young girls were astonished. Vivian asked, "Do you ever want to be popular? If so, change your report!" Brianna asked, "Do you ever want to sit in the back of the bus with the cool kids? If so, change your report." Ashley asked, "Do you ever want to have more than one friend? If so, change your report." Vivian grabbed her green and white world cup soccer ball and handed it to Ashley, like a herd of desperately fleeing gazelles, Ashley and Brianna flew down the stairs and out the door.

Valerie sat there and thought about what the three young ladies had said to her. "I want to be popular! I want to sit in the back of the bus with the cool kids! I want more than one friend!" Valerie said to herself. "Who needs honesty? Who needs sincerity? Who needs integrity?" she asked herself. Valerie opened her laptop and erased what she had written as she questioned herself "Why? Why, did I listen to that bad, bad man Mr. Dulany?"

Monday

The Masked Model

Monday morning, dreaded by many, but a necessary part of the week for without Monday morning, you would not have Wednesday, or Friday afternoon, but it was here. With the help of her sister Vivian, Valerie finished her report, or should I say her fantasy story about the events at the hospital last week. The story mentioned how disorganized and unprofessional the hospital staff were and without Valerie, Parkview hospital would have fallen into a deeper state of despair. Thank goodness, Valerie with her red cape and superpowers were there to save the day. Valerie was proud, she even included images with her report, something she learned working last year in Mrs. Marino's fifth grade class at Hallsberry School.

The big yellow bus, number 452, came and stopped at the corner of Joyce and Terry Road. Valerie was ready for the laughing, the bullying and the harassment that was about to come. Clemente, the bus driver, opened the side door and greeted Valerie, "Hi Valerie, missed you last week, how was the hospital training?" Valerie sat in the seat behind Clemente and sadly remarked "Great."

It was eerily quiet on the bus ride to the middle school, the cool kids in the back of the bus were relentless in their pursuit of being the perfect bullies. Whether they were teasing someone, picking on someone or insulting someone they never stopped, but today there was nothing. Valerie was mystified, but would curiosity ruin the nice ride to the middle school, did she dare look back?

Curiosity got the best of Valerie. She tried to stay under the radar, but the bullies always found a way to pick on Valerie. In elementary school, the students knew they could always go to Mr. Dulany, or any other adult and they would put an immediate and permanent end to the bullying. Mr. Dulany had a zero tolerance for anyone who even attempted to be a bully.

Once he was told of someone bullying, he was like a bull in a china shop. Fiercely, he would immediately talk with the suspected bully and like magic, it would stop. But the middle school was different, there was no Mr. Dulany, and the bullies seem to be bigger and meaner. Valerie bravely looked back, there was no Camilla, there was no Amari, the bully leaders were gone. Valerie breathed a sigh of relief. This could be the best ride ever. Soon bus 452, pulled up to the front entrance of the middle school, as usual there was twenty other buses with several hundred other young students coming to school. Valerie really was invisible.

There was nothing special about this school day. English was boring, they talked about a new book called "Valerie and the Beanstalk", but Valerie had nothing to contribute because she had never read it. Rumor was it was an excellent action-packed story, Valerie promised the teacher she would read it one day. Valerie did well in Algebra, the graphing, the equations, it all came so easy. But there was art class, Valerie loved painting and was considered very talented. She promised Mr. Dulany she would paint a picture for him one day.

Lunch was okay, Monday was pizza day, nothing like the hospitals but still pizza day. Valerie never got tired of her pepperoni and pineapple pizza, but after lunch came the assembly. Each student who earned a week-long field trip would be giving their report on what happened, and what they learned about their prospective career choices. Valerie had received a preview program of the assembly. The principal, Dr. Higgenbotham decided to start off with the most exciting person, Amari and his football week, followed by Camilla and her beautiful cover shoot. Valerie was scheduled to report last.

It was 1:00, lunch was over and the middle school students were starting to migrate to the new theatre. It was a state-of-the-art theatre, not a gym turned into a "theatre". There was professional lighting, real working microphones, excellent acoustics, this was the real McCoy. Valerie was nervous, her stomach started to rumble, however she did not see any of the other presenters. She wondered where they were.

Valerie sat with the rest of her class clutching her "report". She scanned the theatre for William, Joseline, and Sophia, she did not see any of them. Next Valerie looked for Amari, Camilla and Amiya, she saw nothing, quickly scanning the room again Valerie saw nothing. Back and forth, back and forth her eyes went, nothing. She began to worry, asking hers "Did they forget about me again?"

Suddenly the small orchestra began the music, indicating it was time for the assembly to begin. Everyone sat down and was quiet, Mrs. Suarez elegantly walked up to the podium and greeted the students, "Good afternoon Middle School students, Welcome to our first annual Career Week Celebration!" The students applauded and cheered. "Hosting this fabulous event will be our beloved Principal, Dr. Higgenbotham!". Once again, the students cheered as the principal proudly walked across the stage towards the big brown wooden podium. The students continued to cheer wildly for their beloved principal.

Dr. Higgenbotham smiled and waved to his adoring fans. The middle school students loved him, he was kind and caring. He took very good care of his students and was known for knowing each one by name. "Good afternoon, students!" he proudly started. "Without further ado, I give you the participants in our first annual Career Fair" the students cheered and applauded as the students began to walk out on stage.

"First we have Amari" (he walked out on stage). The crowd cheered as he sat down on the first green rusty folding chair. "Next we have the next material girl Camilla." She came up on stage wearing a large hat, waved and sat down next to Amari." The crowd cheered. "Then we have William, Joseline and Sophia. The crowd cheered. However, the girl sitting next to Valerie, Emma leaned over and whispered to Valerie, "Shouldn't you be up there too?" Valerie realized her friend Emma was right, she was supposed to be up there with the other participants, but the school forgot about her, again. Valerie was invisible. Valerie grabbed her report and hustled her way backstage.

Dr. Higgenbotham continued reading the names as the students paraded across the stage holding their reports. "Next we have Amiya, and last but not least we have Valerie." The crowd cheered as the principal asked Mrs. Suarez who Valerie was. Mrs. Suarez did not know either. Amiya walked across the stage followed by a very late Valerie. Surprised at the little girl the principal rudely asked, "That's Valerie?"

The crowd continued to cheer. The participants each holding their report waited anxiously to give their report. Valerie's mind wandered," Speak with honesty, think with sincerity and act with integrity?" Valerie tried to get those words out of her mind but couldn't, thanks to that bad, bad man Mr. Dulany.

Dr. Higgenbotham introduced his first guest, all American athlete Amari. The crowd went wild as Amari strutted to the podium. Amari started to speak, "It was a tough week, but let me introduce my mentor for the week Justin Fields starting quarterback of the Chicago Bears." Justin Fields came out from the right stage curtain on crutches, Justin had a broken right fibula. The crowd was shocked. Justin Fields waved as he came to stand by Amari. Then Amari rolled up the left side of his blue flannel shirt to reveal a cast, he had broken his humorous bone in two places. The crowd was shocked.

In order to make Justin Fields more comfortable Dr. Higgenbotham asked Mrs. Suarez to get a chair for the superstar, she replied "There aren't any more!" Pointing to Valerie he abruptly commanded, "Take it from Tamara, she can stand!" Mrs. Suarez swiftly took the chair from underneath Valerie. Valerie was not shocked; this was her life.

Amari continued to talk, "Today I come before you humbled by my experience as a Chicago Bear. I must and will be honest." Valerie heard the word honest and thought about what Mr. Dulany had said "speak with honesty." Valerie wanted to throw up. Amari continued talking about his experience, I thought I was the greatest thing since sliced bread, but I was wrong."

"This week was a nightmare, I tried tackling the 300-pound linebackers and got crushed, flattened to the ground like a pancake. I tried defense but they ran circles around me scoring constantly. Arrogantly, I thought I was a great quarterback, but I spent most of the time flattened on the ground, I was sacked, rushed and hurried, it was embarrassing. By Friday I was so aggravated and had to prove myself, so I broke the rules, and some bones."

"After the whistle blew, I took a cheap shot at Justin Fields, broke his leg and my arm, sidelining both of us 4-6 weeks." The crowd was silent. "I have learned that I need to stay in school and take my lessons seriously, in case of injury. I have learned while sports are fun, it is not the only thing in life. I may be good, but I have a long, long way to go before thinking I am ready for the big leagues." Amari paused and smiled, "Thanks Mr. Fields for everything and sorry for the broken leg!" Justin and Amari hugged each other and worked their way off the stage.

The students gave Amari and Justin a standing ovation. Valerie was given her chair back and sat down. She thought to herself, "A bad week?

He deserves it." Almost jealous, Valerie told herself, "I can't wait to hear Camilla's awesome week with Kylie Jenner. Dr. Higgenbotham smiled and spoke into the microphone, "What a nice young man!" Continuing, Dr. Higgenbotham began to introduce the beautiful Camilla. Valerie wanted to throw up.

"Next, from our career fair is Camilla, the school's most beautiful student, sunshine to the world." Shyly, bashfully a young lady wearing Levi jeans and an oversized grey sweatshirt started walking across the stage. Adjusting her large over-sized hat to cover her face, Camilla was being unusually bashful. Dr. Higgenbotham was very suspicious. Still hiding mercifully behind her over-sized straw hat, Camilla finally made it to the podium. The crowd was flabbergasted.

"Hello fellow middle school students, I had a great week modeling thank you! Kylie Jenner was my mentor!" Kylie Jenner walked out on stage the crowd cheered. Camilla grabbed Kylie's hand and tried leaving. Dr. Higgenbotham quickly commanded the ladies to stop. Tired of this malarkey, Principle, Dr. Higgenbotham decided to stop this charade. Without thinking, without warning, without a concern, Dr. Higgenbotham grabbed the hat off Camilla's head. Mrs. Suarez was shocked, the principal chuckled, and the students started to laugh hysterically. Valerie wanted to throw up.

Camilla was wearing a special green medicated beauty mask. It was full of nutrients designed to help with sagging skin, baggy eyes, large pores and many other imperfections of the face. Trying to be brave and trick her audience of fellow middle schoolers, Camilla started to speak but was rudely interrupted by her conscious. Pausing for a millisecond, Camilla openly shared with her peers that she wanted to think with sincerity. Valerie wanted to throw up, thinking about what Mr. Dulany said.

Camilla continued speaking even though many of the boys heckled her and her green mask. Speaking over the crude boys, Camilla started her speech, "Today I stand before you, a failure as a super model. I come humbly before you, I have just spent one of the worst weeks of my life." Pausing for a moment and taking a huge breath, she continued to tell her audience that there were at least fifty incredibly gorgeous girls there at the big downtown modeling studio and this made Camilla very nervous.

Quickly the nervousness turned to anxiety and sweat, causing the hormones in her body to go wild. The anxiety sweat and hormones rapidly turned in a giant pimple on her picture-perfect pretty nose. With her first photo shoot in under an hour, the pimple was popped, it was a gusher, and the makeup artist covered it with a revolutionary new blush and powder that would make the huge pimple on her nose invisible. Jas, the make-up artist applied it freely on Camilla's perfect face.

Within seconds after the application of the new cover up, Camilla's face began to tingle. Camilla was excited, she thought the new cover-up was working. Jas was excited, now she could make anybody look gorgeous with her experimental new cover up. Jas was going to be a millionaire all thanks to Camilla and her pus-filled pimple. Camilla got in front of the professional cameramen with her flowing hair, high heels and exclusive one-of-kind Eve St. Clair designer gown and struck a pose.

The tingling on her face soon turned to pain, the pain turned to a severe itch, the itch turned into a burning sensation, the burning sensation quickly transformed into an indescribable over the top, unbearable inferno on her face. Screaming in pain, Camilla was brought to the woman's washroom to wash off Jas's million-dollar idea. Jas was not going to be a millionaire today, or tomorrow. The pain was unbearable, and Camilla was eventually brought to Northwestern Hospital in Chicago for observation.

"Today I come before you and tell you I am not ready to be a model. Although my face will eventually heal with this all-natural solution of guacamole, cucumbers, spinach and mayonnaise, I have decided to stay in school and take school more seriously, for now I have learned beauty comes and goes. Thank you, Kylie Jenner for giving me this incredible opportunity." The crowd cheered as Camilla and Kylie Jenner cat walked off the stage.

With a tear in his eye, Dr. Higgenbotham came back to the podium, Mrs. Suarez handed the principal a Kleenex. "That was beautiful! "Declared Dr. Higgenbotham. "We should all be as sincere as Camilla." The crowd applauded once again in appreciation of her sincerity. Valerie wanted to throw up. "Moving things forward, let me introduce William. William spent a week working at the McDonald's on Army trail road learning the fast-food business." The audience applauded William as he and his mentor, the Manager of the McDonald's, Naomi Smith, came to the podium, both wearing their yellow, red and black uniforms. William wore his special "trainee" name badge complete with the golden arches on it.

Naomi started to speak first, "I would like to say that it was a very rough week for William and me, but no matter what happened, William acted with integrity everyday no matter what the assignment of the day was. On Monday he acted with integrity, on Tuesday, Wednesday, Thursday, and Friday he acted with integrity." The crowd cheered and applauded William, Valerie wanted to throw up.

Then it hit Valerie, everybody else brought their mentors. Valerie was never told to bring Miss Llivia. Valerie hated being invisible, she was always left off the lists, the principal didn't even know her name, life sucked as the invisible girl. Valerie would have to lie to cover up the missing Miss Llivia.

Continuing his speech, William continued, "Yes, I had a terrible week. Yes, I made mistakes, constantly, but acting with integrity, I bravely went into work every day. On Monday, I fried the hamburgers and grilled the fries. On Tuesday, I forgot to turn on the timer for the fries, causing a small fire and an unexpected visit from the Glenside fire department. With Wednesday's delivery, I put the paper cups, napkins and Styrofoam containers in the freezer and the frozen hamburger patties and frozen

French fries in dry unrefrigerated storage. On Thursday, the Manager put me on customer service, I mixed up so many orders that we lost count. On Friday, they put me on clean-up duty outside. Let me say the insurance companies will be busy for a while."

The Manager, Naomi Smith, took over the presentation. "The fast-food industry is a tough place to work. At McDonald's, a 37.5 billion dollar a year company, 75 burgers a second are sold, and every 14.5 hours a new McDonald's is opened, it is a challenging job. It's demanding, when the company serves and feeds 65 million people a day and is the largest toy supplier in the world. But when you make a mistake or two or three, customers are quick to get angry and belittle you, let alone the staff and management, but everyday William came into work and acted with integrity."

The crowd cheered for William. William began to speak again, "After I turn 16, Naomi has personally guaranteed me a job when I am ready. Benefits include free meals and tuition assistance for college. The crowd cheered. And before I leave Naomi has graciously brought coupons for a free value meal for everybody." The crowd gave Naomi and William a standing ovation.

William and Naomi left the stage waving. Dr. Higgenbotham came to the stage and sarcastically stated, "Many of you need to try acting with integrity!" Valerie wanted to throw up, hearing those terrible words yet again. "Why? Why, did I listen to that bad, bad man Mr. Dulany?"

The Hidden Report

Valerie gazed at the small clock backstage, it was 2:25, Only 35 minutes before the dismal bell rings. Valerie thought they still had Joseline left with her Fannie Mae chocolate extravaganza, Sophia was left with her week-long journey of beating a pro-gamer and then Amiya and her comedy routine. If she were lucky, time would run out and the assembly would be over. Dr. Higgenbotham continued, "We must continue if we want to finish. We still have Joseline presenting, Sophia presenting and Amiya presenting their week in the world of working. Now without further delay..." Suddenly Mrs. Suarez interrupted Dr. Higgenbotham, "Don't forget about Taylor!"

Dr. Higgenbotham corrected himself, "It seems I left off the young straggly looking girl at the end, Heidy? Without further delay I give you Joseline and her mentor Master Chocolatier Dominga. The Crowd cheered. Valerie had enough, she decided she was going to leave. As Joseline gave her speech Valerie decided she needed to be sick, Valerie suddenly began to cough. Amiya who was sitting next to her said, "Take a cough drop Betsy!" Valerie wanted to throw up.

With master chocolatier Dominga standing beside her, Joseline began her speech. "My week was filled with many obstacles, but like my fellow middle schoolers I decided to go through them instead of under or over them." Valerie coughed again causing Joseline to lose her place, the audience stared. Dr. Higgenbotham said can somebody get Kristine a cough drop?" Being invisible sucked. Mrs. Suarez handed Valerie a cough drop.

Joseline continued, "making chocolate is a gift, an art and I my friends do not have the gift, on Monday I made chocolate charcoal, on Tuesday I made chocolate water." Valerie coughed again, Dr. Higgenbotham gave Valerie the evil eye. Valerie decided this was the perfect time to escape, she abruptly stood up and started walking toward the exit, however on the first step Valerie tripped on the white shoelaces on her cool blue fashion gym shoes.

Falling clumsily to the hard theatre stage floor, Valerie was aggravated. Not wanting to risk further embarrassment, Valerie quickly returned to her seat. Like a miracle from heaven Valerie stopped coughing and quickly tied her long white shoelaces. Unfortunately adding insult to injury, Dr. Higgenbotham asked Valerie, "Are we done Emily?" Valerie shook her head yes.

Joseline continued with her story, "On Wednesday Dominga asked me to mix cocoa powder into the sugar mix, I thought I heard Cocoa Puffs. By Thursday they had me packaging the fancy chocolate bars. Personally, I think I mixed the wrappers up, I think I put the almond wrapper on the plain bar, the jelly wrapper on the almond bar and the plain wrapper on the jelly bar."

"On Friday, Dominga had me loading the candy and chocolate bars in the trucks. I am almost positive I sent the lollipops and hard candy to the Sahara Desert warehouse and the gourmet chocolate bars to the warehouse just south of the Arctic Circle, almost positive." Suddenly Dominga looked like she was going to throw up.

Like a bolt of lightning, Dominga ran off the stage. Joseline took a bow, said "Thank you!" and began strolling off the stage. Valerie got nervous. Unexpectedly, Joseline came back and proudly stated "By the way, everyone will get a chocolate bar at the end of the assembly." The crowd was quiet. Joseline swiftly replied, "the ones made by Dominga, not me!" The crowd erupted in a loud outburst of gratefulness.

Dr. Higgenbotham quickly came to the podium and encouraged the students to settle down for they still had three more presenters, Amiya the comic, Sophia, the gamer, and Mary. Valerie wanted to throw up. The crowd cheered. Without further delay let me give you the one the only class jokester Amiya, who spent an entire week working with different comics at the famous comedy club Second City. The crowd cheered as Amiya walked onto the theatre stage.

Amiya walked up to the podium and began to talk, "I come before you today having quite the successful week. I worked with many different performers at the Comedy Club. However, for some odd reason they said I was very special and didn't want to take credit for my talent. So, I don't have a mentor, nor will I be handing out free meals or free candy bars." The crowd was quiet with thoughts of sorrow. Amiya continued "Even though most of the comics suggested with my unique talent I sign up for the Siberian Comedy Tour, I declined so I could share a few jokes for you!" The crowd was mystified, Dr. Higgenbotham was weary, and Valerie was excited, time was running out.

"R.I.P. boiled water, you will be Mist!" Amiya said. The crowd was quiet. Amiya continued, "Don't trust atoms, they make up everything." Only Mr. King the science teacher laughed. "I was addicted to the Hokey Pokey, but now I turned myself around" Amiya snickered. "Most people are shocked when they find out I am a bad electrician," Amiya joked. The crowd was relentless in their silence.

Saving her best jokes for last Amiya composed herself, smiled and started telling jokes, "Don't spell part backwards, it's a trap." A pin dropped and it was heard by everyone. Continuing Amiya said, "Thanks for explaining many to me, it means a lot." Tired of the bad jokes Jose' stood up and yelled, "Got an air freshener? Your jokes stink!" Totally unphased Amiya bravely continued.

"I started with nothing, thank goodness I saved, and I have most of it left." Still nothing, except a noisy cricket in the far back corner of the theatre. Dr. Higgenbotham realized this was the Titanic and was going to give Amiya one more chance, before she hit the iceberg. In a last-ditch effort, Amiya tried one more time, "I am reading a really good book about gravity, it's really hard to put down."

Dr. Higgenbotham was too late, the Titanic hit the iceberg and was going down. Anonymous students yelled, "Stay in school you need it, stay off Jokes, they are bad for you." Dr. Higgenbotham threw her a life preserver, "Sorry Amiya, time is running out, we only have ten minutes, and we still have Sophia and Brianna to present their reports." Valerie was invisible, Valerie was forgettable, Valerie wanted to throw up.

Amiya, still smiling, was shocked that her presentation was being cut short, the crowd was just warming up to her. She thanked the crowd and exited, stage right. Dr. Higgenbotham approached the podium, next up we have Sophia our future professional gamer. Sophia spent many hours alone on her computer playing Minecraft, she had very little social skills and very little patience, but she was the envy of every amateur video gamer in the theatre. The crowd cheered.

Alone and scared, Sophia came bashfully to the podium. She looked down, never making eye contact with the audience. Sophia stood there as the crowd of students waited earnestly for her to give them the juicy details of an exciting week of being with a professional gamer. In the blink of an eye Sophia gave her report.

"On Monday, I went thinking I was an excellent gamer, by Friday I changed my career path and would like to be an accountant. The Professional gamer, George Thompson, beat me easily every day. He hid in biomes where I never found him, he used creepers that seemed bigger and stronger than mine. His enderman was always quicker than mine and when I did find him, he used his nether to hide again. I don't know where he got his power pickaxe or his powerful redstone, it was frustrating!" said Sophia.

"So frustrating, I "accidently" threw a controller at Mr. Thompson on Friday, he refused to come today because of the "accident", something about me having a bad temper." Sophia quickly left. The crowd cheered.

Dr. Higgenbotham came to the microphone and began to articulate, "Our last presenter, Chloe? Was a whatever?" The crowd was baffled at this new girl, Chloe? Betsy? Heidy? Whoever she was.

Valerie was embarrassed. She began to wonder why she signed up for this humiliation. As she walked to the podium, she held her "report" in her tiny hands and asked herself "Why, why, did I listen to that bad, bad man Mr. Dulany?"

The Covered
Consequences

Valerie composed herself, she looked out at the audience and remembered what Mr. Dulany had said to her, "Speak with Honesty, Think with Sincerity, Act with Integrity." Valerie was quiet as she saw the hundreds of eyes staring at her. Opening her report slowly, Valerie thought about how honest Amari and Camilla were, they too had incredibly bad weeks. William made the McDonald's a nightmare for the week for his manager Naomi Smith. Joseline caused havoc for five days for Dominga, but both thought about their work with sincerity. Sophia and Amiya failed miserably in their quest to be the best, but they acted with integrity when they read their reports.

"There's still time for me to become visible!" Valerie exclaimed inside her brain. "With this story, I will become belle of the ball, people will know me for having the best week ever. I will become popular by telling my "story". This story will change my life!" Dr. Higgenbotham was watching the clock and quickly reminded Christy to give her presentation. She opened her report and began reading the report.

Deceitfully, Valerie started her presentation. Unfortunately, my mentor, Miss Llivia, is not able to attend this assembly. However, I spent the entire week learning many different areas of Parkview Hospital. I have learned that a patient's health and recovery depend on many people and departments throughout the hospital. During my stay I worked at the reception desk, in the cafeteria, in the landscaping department, in the custodial department and spent time being a candy striper."

Suddenly one tall boy from the audience yelled out, "Ashley, Joseline was a candy maker!" Another dark-haired young lady, "Take a hint Mila, nobody wanted to keep you around." Valerie smiled and tried to continue. Running out on stage came Miss Llivia, "Sorry everybody, busy, busy, busy."

"Sorry Miss Llivia, we have two minutes before we have to end this assembly. Can you and Leah please finish your presentation?" Miss Llivia was confused wondering who Leah was but replied "sure." Miss Llivia continued, "Today I come to present Valerie," she was rudely interrupted by Dr. Higgenbotham asking "Who's Valerie?" "To present Valerie with the Employee of the Year Award"

Dr. Higgenbotham was shocked, the students were shocked, and Valerie was shocked. Valerie? Employee of the Year Award? Miss Llivia continued, "Because of Valerie being with us last week, today we are a better hospital." Valerie thought she was being pranked and looked around for the television cameras. Miss Llivia handed Valerie the plaque and certificate proclaiming Valerie the "Employee of the Year", shook her hand and gave her a huge hug.

Unexpectantly Dr. Higgenbotham yelled out, "That's my girl, Valerie!" A young man named Joey, who was in her advanced placement science class, yelled out, "That's my best friend, Valerie!" Another younger boy who Valerie saw on the bus every morning, named Justin, hollered, "That's my neighbor Valerie, we grew up together." A skinny Latina girl, who Valerie sat across from at the loser's lunch table, but never said a word to Valerie screamed, "Way to go Valerie!" Suddenly the whole theatre started chanting "Valerie! Valerie! Valerie". Valerie wanted someone to pinch her to make sure she wasn't dreaming again.

PART THREE

With time running out, Dr, Higgenbotham requested sternly that the students settle down so Valerie could finish her "report". Thinking about what she had written in her "report", she wisely handed the microphone to Miss Llivia. Her report was more like a story full of lies, deceit and dishonesty. Valerie did not speak with honesty, think with sincerity or act with integrity when she wrote her report. Valerie was disappointed in herself.

Miss Llivia apologized for being late, she had to pick up the special gold-plated mahogany plaque and got stuck in construction traffic on North Avenue. Watching the clock very closely, Mrs. Suarez reminded Miss Llivia she had less than two minutes to finish, otherwise, the children would miss their buses.

"We didn't know what to expect when the hospital was asked to mentor a student for a future career as a nurse. What we did get was a Valerie, a sweet naïve young lady who might change her mind as time progressed, who came in everyday with a smile on her face and a positive can-do attitude."

She was a receptionist on Monday, busy place, first impression of the hospital, starting today with have two people working there, better customer service, and we have ordered reusable maps for the visitors. On Tuesday, she worked in the busy cafeteria with Elena. This week we have signs that ask customers to throw away their trash and effective immediately no children should be left alone in the cafeteria, unfortunately the cafeteria staff are not babysitters.

On Wednesday, Valerie worked outside with Esmeralda and Aisha, where she taught them how to plant bulbs. Effective immediately, when something is broken, like the water spigot we fix it immediately, no more rigging it to temporarily have it working. On Thursday, Valerie worked with Soha keeping the hospital clean, a tough unappreciated job that Soha tries to have fun with. Effective immediately, the trash company is required to have a replacement dumpster when they take our dumpster, no more leaving it outside for the animals to scavenge through.

Finally, we have learned that we have pushed Isabella too far in her candy striping duties. Candy stripers are supposed to be there to deliver, talk, and laugh with the patients. Thanks to a patient, Mr. Hernandez, he liked it when Valerie spent time talking with him in his room. Effective immediately, Isabella and Jeannette and Andrea' can slow down and spend time talking with the patients. Thanks to Valerie we are expanding our candy striper program." Surprisingly, the end of the day school bell rang.

Like a stampede of wildebeest running from an African cheetah, the children quickly exited the modern theatre joyful another school day was over. Grabbing their jackets, laptops and cell phones from their tiny steel lockers, the homeward bound students ran to the buses hoping to land in their favorite seats. Meanwhile Valerie and Miss Llivia remained in the theatre talking.

"Valerie," Miss Llivia gracefully said. "I know you had a rough week it seems all the students did. The workplace is tough, although you did make it interesting. Your job right now is to stay in school and learn as much as you can. Experience life. Go to school. I promise you a job as a nurse if you get a proper education and get a nursing license. But" Miss Llivia hesitated. Curiosity got the best of Valerie, "What? But What?" she boldly asked.

"I would like you to stay on as a candy striper, volunteer when you can as often or as little as you want. Mr. Hernandez said it was nice talking to you. He said you made him feel comfortable, almost like he knew you his entire life. Mr. Hernandez was upset when Isabella pulled you out of his room. You have a real gift with people, so would you stay on as a candy striper?"

Without hesitation, Valerie jumped up, smiled and screamed "Of course!" Then over the intercom, Mrs. Suarez announced, "Last call for the 3:00 bus, last call for the 3:00 bus. Valerie frantically exclaimed, "have to go!" Valerie ran out of the room and jumped on the bus, where she was greeted with unfamiliar applause and adoration. The middle schoolers chanted, "Valerie! Valerie! Valerie!

The bus driver dropped her by the corner of Joyce and Terry, where she and other students got off the big yellow bus. Unexpectantly April said "See you tomorrow!" Brandon said, "Maybe we can study one day together" and David quietly congratulated her again. Valerie quietly whispered to herself, "I am not invisible! They know my name!" Totally focused on her new-found popularity, Valerie did not see Mr. Dulany trimming his front bushes, Mr. Dulany did not see Valerie either.

With her mother folding the laundry, Valerie ran to her mother and gave her a huge hug and told her about the great day she had, especially with the assembly. Boasting proudly, she told her mom about being asked to continue being a candy striper and she showed her mom the special certificate and plaque that Miss Llivia presented to her. Mom hugged her sweet daughter, and said "I am very proud of you, maybe we can order Panda Express tonight to celebrate."

Relentless in her happiness, Valerie ran to her room to tell everything to her sister Vivian. Valerie said to herself, "Thank Goodness, Thank Goodness, I listened to my good, good friend Mr. Dulany!"

12 Years Later

The Unforeseeable Future

Valerie got out of her old Subaru and strolled through the hospital's parking lot. There were pretty flowers everywhere. Red marigolds, orange marigolds, beautiful red and white roses, day lilies, yellow daisies, the grounds were gorgeous. Esmeralda and Aisha were doing an excellent job with the landscaping.

Approaching the front door to Parkview Hospital, Valerie took one last look at the beautiful flowers and walked in. She was quickly greeted by Maritza, "Can I help you?" Valerie saw the $3.99 Hot dog special sign and laughed. "Yes, I am here to see Miss Llivia about a nursing job. My name is......." Maritza rudely cut her off, "Valerie, you must be the one, the only, the legendary Valerie. You finally decided to work for us. I heard you had job offers from New York, Paris, Chicago, and Los Angeles! I can't believe you chose us!"

"It all started here," Valerie smiled as she talked with Maritza. Miss Llivia quietly walked up to the front desk and hugged her young protégé Valerie." Tell me more, please tell me more" demanded Maritza. "I promise I will make this hiring process short, "replied Miss Llivia, "Then she is all yours." Maritza was excited. "Come on Valerie, let's go to my office" requested Miss Llivia.

PART THREE

Miss Llivia was now the President of Parkview Hospital, and while she had a human resources person to hire and fire people, Miss Llivia wanted to keep her promise made twelve years ago and officially hire Valerie for a nursing job in the hospital. Miss Llivia looked at Valerie and handed her a Lipton Peach Iced Tea, Valerie's favorite. Valerie handed Miss Llivia her impressive resume.

Valerie sat down and drank the cold tea. Looking up on Valerie's bookshelf she saw a fake hairy black spider and a giant striped rattlesnake, also fake, she snickered thinking about Soha. Miss Llivia scanned Valerie's resume, at Glenbard Central High School she took biology, physiology and chemistry. After graduating with honors, Valerie went to Loyola University in Maywood and took courses like sociology and microbiology all while earning a bachelor's degree in nursing. Finally, she was licensed to be a registered nurse with the National Council Licensing Exam where she was ranked in the top 10% of her class. Miss Llivia was impressed, Miss Llivia as promised hired Valerie immediately.

Suddenly there was a knock on the door, it was Ivy, one of Isabella's candy stripers, Ivy handed a balloon with a heart on it to Valerie and handed a balloon with a heart on it to Miss Llivia, both were from Mr. Dulany. Ivy stayed and talked with the two for hours, finally Ivy left, Valerie was impressed with Isabella and her candy stripers. "Want to go to lunch?" asked Miss Llivia. "Elena is serving something new today. Miss Llivia thought to herself "Thank goodness, thank goodness I listened to my good, good friend Mr. Dulany

THE END

Bruce Dulany
Books by Bruce
Chelyw2000@Yahoo.com
January 2022